A WHOLE HEAP OF WISHES

THE WISHING TREE SERIES, BOOK 11

AMANDA PROWSE

PRAISE FOR AMANDA PROWSE

'A powerful and emotional work of fiction' - Piers Morgan

'Deeply moving and emotional, Amanda Prowse handles her explosive subjects with delicate skill' - Daily Mail

'Uplifting and positive, but you will still need a box of tissues' - Hello!

'A gut-wrenching and absolutely brilliant read' - The Irish Sun
'You'll fall in love with this...' - Cosmopolitan

'Deeply moving and eye opening. Powerful and emotional drama that packs a real punch.' - Heat

'Magical' - Now magazine

www.amandaprowse.com
Facebook: https://www.facebook.com/amandaprowsepage
Twitter: @MrsAmandaProwse
Instagram: @MrsAmandaProwse

Published in the United Kingdom by Lionhead Media

ISBN 978-1-915400-01-7 (paperback)
ASIN B09PRR9W7J (eBook)
FIRST EDITION
Cover by Elizabeth Mackey Graphic Design

To everyone who believes in the power of wishes

ALSO BY AMANDA PROWSE

Novels

Poppy Day

What Have I Done?

Clover's Child

A Little Love

Will You Remember Me?

Christmas for One

A Mother's Story

Perfect Daughter

The Second Chance Café (originally *The Christmas Café*)

Three and a Half Heartbeats

Another Love

My Husband's Wife

I Won't Be Home for Christmas

The Food of Love

The Idea of You

The Art of Hiding

Anna

Theo

How to Fall in Love Again (Kitty's Story)

The Coordinates of Loss

The Girl in the Corner

The Things I Know

The Light in the Hallway

The Day She Came Back

An Ordinary Life

Waiting to Begin

To Love and Be Loved

Novellas

The Game

Something Quite Beautiful

A Christmas Wish

Ten Pound Ticket

Imogen's Baby

Miss Potterton's Birthday Tea

Mr Portobello's Morning Paper

I Wish . . .

Memoir

The Boy Between: A Mother and Son's Journey From a World Gone
Grey (with Josiah Hartley)

Women Like Us

CHAPTER 1

*V*era opened her eyes slowly. She'd dreamed of him again. It bothered her. Not the dream itself, no that was lovely, but the fact he still had the power to make her wake feeling... a little off, even after all these years. She ran her hand over the cold side of the bed next to her, able to recall, decades later, what it had felt like to have him radiating heat, the weight of him on the mattress, the sound of his breathing, his irritating snore. But also, how his very presence had made her feel safe, made any place feel like home.

Not that it was real, any of it. The man in her thoughts was frozen in time, as was she in her dream. Maybe that's why she liked it so much, the chance to revisit herself before her skin was a little crêpey, her boobs had slipped on her chest, her eyesight was on the wane and without the aid of a good kohl she had hardly any eyebrows at all. Yes, to spend time with her younger self was nice. Her phone beeped its alarm, as it often did a few seconds after she woke, as if her body clock was programmed to wake anyhow,

'Up and at 'em!' She called out, fracturing the silence that she knew could become something quite invasive if she didn't voice her inner monologue and keep the threatening demons of loneliness at bay.

With her morning rituals complete, shower taken, hair set, make up on, breakfast of toast and orange juice devoured, she stepped out onto her deck and looked up, welcoming the feel of the glorious May sunshine on her face. Mornings like this felt like a gift, a big old cup of warmth when her body had been used to shivering a little at night. She loved these days when the world changed course and ploughed straight on through 'til summer without stopping. It spoke of hope and that was no bad thing.

Gathering her plastic watering can, full of rain, she tended to the mismatched pots that lined her porch, giving each a healthy drink and a word or two of encouragement which she figured did no harm. She then checked her mailbox. It was a delight to find a letter that wasn't a bill, or junk mail. Pulling the pale envelope from the dark confines, she stopped short on the path. Her heart raced and the breath stuttered in her throat as excitement fizzed in her veins. She read and re-read the return address.

'Ithaca,' it could only mean one thing, *Knox*.

Exhaling slowly, her face broke into a smile at the sound of his name in her thoughts. Popping the letter into her purse, she decided to open it at work while the tea kettle boiled, giving her time to savour every written word, every dot, and every dash, before her first customer of the day. Rushing through it now would be unsatisfactory, like having to abandon a cup of tea that had got to the exact right temperature or leaving a theatre to catch the bus and miss the last ten minutes of a show. No, she would take her time. There was something wonderful about knowing she had his words to look forward to, like a pretty box of chocolates waiting to be unwrapped and devoured, or a movie recorded and waiting to be watched. The anticipation was often as good as the event itself. If not better.

With a spring in her step, she almost danced back into her trailer. Having maneuvered into the narrow gap between the wall and bed in the small room, she sidled along to pull the lacey coverlet, which sat over the foot of her bed, taut and plump the array of pillows that rested against the padded headboard. It was a tight space, an uncomfortable venture, but worth it. She liked to come home after a long day of doing hair color and updos and see her bedroom looking pretty. Remembering the days of her childhood when the shared mattress was greasy and bare, and the windows covered with paper in lieu of drapes. Here in her little haven, the bed covers were silky, lace edged and lilac with more accent pillows than one head could possibly need.

Nestling their tiny bodies against the headboard sat her beloved dolls, whose outfits were all hand stitched, along with the fancy big hats and parasols that made up their accessories. Vera spoke to these porcelain-faced dolls too, gently wiping dust from their faces with the kiss of a soft cloth. Miss Madeleine, Miss Charlotte, Miss Emilia-Jane, and Miss Jannette, how she doted on them.

'Pretty as a peach in June.'

She smiled at them, before refolding the hand towel by the sink in the bathroom to ensure the floral embroidered edge was on display. It mattered little that she lived alone and that no one would get to see the fruits of her attentive labours, still she liked to leave her abode just so. With the galley kitchen sparkling, the fringed rug in front of the couch straightened, and not a speck of dust on the shelves around her wide TV, everything was just right. It was important to her. Her trailer was small, some would say cluttered but not Vera, she would describe it as, 'a place for everything and everything in its place'.

She had learned at a young age that there was no scratched surface, no water marked wood or stained area that couldn't be brightened with the addition of a crocheted doily and a vibrant display of faux flowers. To step inside her home was akin to walking into a florist's shop, albeit without the glorious heady scent of fresh blooms that greeted you at Bertie Petals in town. Not that she didn't do her best to recreate that smell via the burning of fragrant candles and a good squirt of Febreze Floral Gardens.

As a child growing up in the Deep South, peering into the windows of other houses in the suburb she called home was one of her very favourite things. How she would marvel at the white gauzy drapes that fluttered in the breeze, the checkered red and white tablecloths that graced the tops of kitchen tables and the cinnamon scented, golden crusted apple pies that sat cooling on windowsills, awaiting a spoon and a curl of vanilla ice cream. How she longed with her heart and soul to live in a house like that. Her parent's home was very different. The wooden fence was broken, the grass gone to expose hard dirt, the front door barely fitted the frame, and the yard was covered in dog shit. They didn't even have a dog. Her childhood self was wrapped tightly in a cloak of shame that on the rare occasion anyone saw inside her mother's house, threatened to suffocate her.

Inside it wasn't much better. The whole place was cluttered with junk, piled up around the large La-Z-boys. Old newspapers, garbage, empty soup cans, dirty cat bowls encrusted with food, sticky floors, and greasy cushions. The whole place stank, and she could smell the whiff of fried food on her clothes and in her hair even on the day after bath night. It was as if that stink lived in the very fibre of her being and it would take more than soap or detergent to wash it away. Not that she realised at the time just how very poor they were. This realisation came when she left home, visited other people's houses and was able to make the stark comparison.

It saddened her that this was her overriding memory of growing up, and at different times she put the state of the place down to her momma being poor, being sick, being depressed, but the end result was just the same. That house was as dirty as a ditch and that was the truth. Not that she didn't view her momma's situation without sympathy. It can't have been easy. Her daddy was a drunk and not the funny, jovial kind, but a mean one with a quick fist and a poison tongue. Her older brothers liked two things in life: hunting and fighting. The latter they would indulge in in the yard and in the lounge of their shotgun home and more often than not, covered in the blood and mud that their clothes had accrued while partaking in the former.

'For the love of Jesus Christ will you two quit?' this her momma's favoured refrain as her bulky brothers crashed and bashed, kicking holes in doors as they went, knocking thin framed floral pictures from the walls, and landing hard knuckled thumps on each other's faces and heads that resulted in the bruises and cuts they wore as battle scars.

It was a life riven with this low level of violence. The shouting, the hollering, the drinking, the breaking of bottles, the gunfire, the blood of rabbits or the odd razorback dripping onto the porch from where they were hung and gutted. And her mother, slowly sinking deeper and deeper into the chair that was her seat, her throne, her whole wide world. It was from here she yelled with one pudgy hand on the remote control, trying to keep order over the shitty kingdom where money, space and affection were all in short supply.

Despite her less than favourable start in life, Vera was a little girl who grew up with fairy tales dancing behind her eyelids every night in the warm cocoon of southern heat. Her meemaw, an oasis of kindness in the turbulent sands of her life, would rock her gently on the porch swing. And as the crickets chirped their night song, she'd fall asleep to tales of princesses and faraway lands, of warm seas and desert islands, of big whales and friendly fish and of winning! As in these stories, the good, fair, and kind always, always triumphed. It was a nice place for her mind to reside, among the pages where anything was possible if you just *wished hard enough*! Far nicer than listening to her daddy come home with a gutful of moonshine and the sound of her momma whimpering as she crawled from the floor toward her marital bed, where one time, an unfortunate 'slip' had caused her wrist to snap like a twig. And on another, she heard her cry softly, as she lowered her body onto the La-Z-Boy, her cheek seeking out a soft cushion, after stupidly 'walking into' a door frame in the dark, what a corker that black eye was! It made young Vera resolve to always have a night light on lest such a fate might befall her. She never wanted a door frame to do that to *her* eye. True to her word, Vera who had slept alone for more nights that she hadn't in all her years on the planet, still kept a night light glowing in the hallway. For just in case.

Yes, it was important to Vera to keep her trailer home as neat as a pin. *Pride.*

'S'all about pride!' She reminded her plants. That's what Billy used to say, but then Billy used to say a lot of things…

Had anyone been aware of her background, they would understand her determination to make life pretty. Her philosophy was simple; the prettier you made it, the prettier it seemed. Indeed, her mantra was, 'aint nothing a little curl and lipstick can't cure!' The idea served her well when tending to the beauty needs and hair requirements of the ladies of Linden Falls at her salon, 'Curl Up and Dye'. It also extended to her personally, where her sunny personality, positive platitudes and warm welcome to all, hid a deeper, private sadness.

Closing her front door, she hitched the raffia bag over her narrow shoulder and spied her neighbour, Mrs Kenny, sitting out front, as she liked to do on days like this before the heat got up and she sought out the tepid water of the hot tub, which her nephew Randall had installed on the rear deck.

'Good morning, Mrs Kenny!' Vera waved.

'Morning, dear! Thought I'd get a head start. It's gonna be a warm one!'

Vera noted she was topping and tailing green beans and lobbing them into a big old red plastic bowl by her feet.

'You got the right idea.'

'Hope you don't mind me saying, Vera, but what in the name of God have you done to your hair?'

'You like it?' She patted the pin curls that hung down around her slender neck, aware of the bouffant poodle effect that sat on a heap on top. The colour had been described on the side of the bottle as blush, but the effect was more magenta. Yep, no doubt about it, it was definitely magenta.

'You did that on purpose?' the woman held her paring knife still and her mouth fell open a little. It did little to give Vera confidence that this colour was a good idea. Not that it mattered, she could easily fix it with a new colour any time she chose.

'I did indeed.' She beamed her megawatt smile.

'We'll see you coming home in the dark, your head's lit up like a Christmas tree on Main Street!'

Vera laughed loudly and heartily as she was wont to do, quashing images of Christmas as she did so. Most folk, she knew, loved the holidays, but not her. For her it was a time of sadness, when her thoughts wandered to what might have been and the sweetest memories came back to taunt her like a sharp stick in the gut. Not that she had to worry about that right now, it was nearly summertime.

'I'll take that as a compliment Mrs Kenny!' she chuckled, as she made her way along the lane, heading out towards the long road and up across into Town Square. 'You have a good day!'

'You too honey!' the old woman went back to her beans.

Linden Falls had been Vera's home for the last decade. Nestling in the glorious state of Vermont, she liked the air up here, it was restorative, nectar for her soul! She also loved the heat in the summer, not as fierce or relentless as she'd known in the south. The snow in wintertime held for her a fascination sparkling like diamonds wherever it lay. And the myriad of golds and russets that lined her walk, to and from the salon in the fall, was nothing short of breathtaking. She loved that big old Linden tree upon which people came from far and wide to tie their wishes. But mostly she loved the other folk who lived here. Sure, it was a cutesy town with Instaworthy vistas on every corner, but it was also one where the community spirit; its beating heart, was strong. A place where she had felt the loving arms of her neighbours surround her, welcoming her, a stranger, into the fold.

The day, she opened her salon, "Curl Up & Dye!" a name chosen in jest that seemed to have stuck, Neva Cabot, owner of the inn, had been one of her first customers. Neva was a woman who was wary and welcoming in equal measure, insisting, as she did to this day, that she was never going to cut her long hair, short. Then there was her dear, late friend Margot, owner of Town Books, the book shop where Margot's daughter Paige now lived. She missed Margot still, a real lady, always polite, always kind. Vera smiled, she never would and never could call herself a lady. Not that she was wanton or wayward, nothing like that, but on some days, she felt the stink of the Delaney name cling to her.

Her customers were loyal. Cassie from Claudine's Bistro came in weekly, Paige following in the footsteps of her mother Margot, Leo who used to own White Cedar Farm and now lived closer to town with her husband Walt, and Loretta, when she was in town and not flitting around doing whatever it was that she did when she disappeared for days or weeks. They had all made appointments in those first weeks, whether supporting the new venture or checking her out it was impossible to know, but either way, they had sat nattering as if they had known her for years and in truth, she couldn't imagine living anywhere else.

Even newcomers like Verity the sparkly Brit was now a regular customer, and Neva too of course and lovely Pam Olson; Linden Falls, it seemed, had a huge capacity for love that made people never want to leave. That and the intimacy of working in a salon meant barriers were broken down quickly, turning customers into friends. It seemed that with a towel on their head and a cup of coffee in their palms, people felt relaxed enough to talk of what irked them, what worried them and what made them happy. Neva might be known as the keeper of wishes, but Vera knew that her role in town life was a vital one, as the keeper of secrets.

Living in the town where the big old wishing tree dominated the square brought her peace. And despite hearing the disregard and doubt in which some held the grand Linden, she wished on it often when her need for guidance or to worship was strong, asking for clarity of thought, forgiveness, sunshine and for the wants and needs of others to be met. And of course, health and happiness for Knox, always that. She figured it wasn't too much different from praying, which had been ever present in her life. It was her belief that God could hear her just as well when she sat in front of the tree as he could if she sat in front of an altar. In fact, the one thing she *did* miss from her childhood was the church.

Raised to love Jesus under a hot tin roof with music that jumped in her veins and where the stomping of feet gave every service the right level of drama, she would never forget the *rhythm* of that worship. Singing, en masse, with legs moving and hands clapping, it lifted her so high she fully expected to one day open her eyes after prayer and find herself with her nose pressed to that old rusting roof where holes meant in bad weather, they had to halt the hymns and position buckets to catch the drips! The rainwater hitting the bucket not enough to put them off their stride or overly interrupt the sermon. Instead, it merely added another dimension to the music that filled the small space, the thrum, thrum, thrum a beat that not only fell from the clouds but seemed to come right from Heaven itself. God's percussion!

Church here in Linden Falls was a more sedate affair; quieter and more ordered. Air-conditioned with neat seating and vast screens on the walls so those at the back didn't miss a thing. For Vera at least, it was without the lasso of fervor that wound itself around her soul and pulled her on and up, out of the darkest times. She pondered, when she first arrived, how Jesus could be so differently admired, but figured faith was like a lot like a menu, sometimes you fancied cheese grits, sometimes steak and eggs, sometimes cherry pancakes, but regardless of your choice, all nourished and filled you right up just the same!

As a new Linden Falls resident, she had arrived in a new skin. No one in this neighborhood knew she was one of the Delaney kids who had lived in *that* house, didn't know she was the daughter of old man Delaney, the drunk, or that she was the sister of the Delaney boys, one now in jail, the other dead, both the end result of too much booze and too little regard for life. It made her sad to think of those men, who she still pictured as little boys, picking up snakes with sticks and chasing each other around the yard. Before they grew up and picked up guns, booze, and fast women.

It also made her sad that her momma and daddy had died without her having seen them for the longest time, but it was the way it had to be. Vera had learned young that self-preservation meant making sometimes difficult choices, Bill had taught her that too. And she'd taken it to heart, knowing that staying away, moving on and rebuilding her life without the Delaney name following in her wake, was how she found happiness and how she survived. As a survivor, and with her outward love of frippery, her fondness of lace and pastels,

Vera was shot through with a spine of steel and the guts of someone mighty, all wrapped in cotton candy colours that fooled the eye into thinking she might be someone soft.

It bothered her that on a sun-filled, beautiful Vermont day like this, she could so easily be taken back to thoughts of her old life.

'Morning Vera!'

Jack Darby called as he loaded up a bucket and a bag of groceries into the back of his flatbed truck. She saw him do a double take when he saw her new hair colour, but ever the gent, said nothing.

'Mornin' Jack, he got you running all over hell's half acre?' she smiled, knowing that he and Verity were about as happy as could be. They were the kind of couple who even made old cynics like her miss the feel of an arm around her waist on a cold night. It was nice, seeing love bloom for the likes of Jack and Verity who were not in the first flush of youth. It gave her hope. Her dream last night had certainly stoked embers that during the waking hours she was sure had burned out. Not that she was looking, no sirree! She stayed clear of all of that, knowing there was just about enough hours in the day to live her life without throwing a man into the mix.

'Yup.' Jack, a man of few words, pulled a face and climbed into his truck.

CHAPTER 2

*V*era knew the joyful anticipation she felt at putting her key in the door and walking inside her own premises would never diminish. It might only be a small salon in a quiet town, but it was quite a thing for a woman like her to be a business owner. And what a pretty little business it was. Three large mirrors, framed with soft-lit lightbulbs sat on the wall with white shelves edged in gold beneath them, and white leather-look chairs that were so comfortable it wasn't unusual for her customers to nod off under the dryer. White and gold trolleys on wheels sat in a row, stuffed full of hair rollers in all different shades of the rainbow, one for every size curl on every sized head, along with combs, brushes, and hair nets to keep those do's looking neat under the dryer. The small crescent shaped counter was also gold and white with a vase full of silk blooms to greet people as they walked in. Out the back was a kitchenette where Mira, her fabulous apprentice of two years, made teas and coffees and loaded up the used towels into the wash-er/dryer on an endless cycle. The kitchenette and salon were linked by a narrow corridor where the lean-back basin was stationed along with glass shelves displaying the various shampoos and conditioners that promised all manner of results. And next to the basin was the ladies room.

With the lights of the salon now gleaming and the blinds pulled up to let the day in, Vera took a minute in the back to grab the letter from her purse. Leaning on the small sink, she slowly placed the envelope under her nose and inhaled. What she expected to smell would have been hard to say, but the fact that his hand had touched this very thing, his fingers had been where hers now lingered. It was as if she might be able to breathe in a small part of him and when you missed someone as much as she did Knox, that was really something. In fact, it was everything. Taking her time, careful not to over rip the envelope or God forbid, damage the letter inside, she carefully slid the paper from its cover and held the two sheets in her palm.

Hey Mom!

Vera looked away, blinking away the tears that gathered on her false lashes, the last thing she wanted was to start the day with her make up all smudged and looking like a racoon. Not that it was easy to control her emotions when just that one word was like a dagger in her chest and conversely a balm for her soul. *Mom...* She was someone's mom, and this was the most precious role that had ever befallen her.

Her eyes scanned the letter, skim reading as was her habit to get the gist, to impatiently hoover up anything of importance, learning whether the content was good or bad, negative, or positive, and bracing herself accordingly, before going back to the beginning and reading again slowly to get the detail. She would then revisit the communique several times, lingering on the style, form, and content, trying to pick up any hidden meaning; clues as to his mood, his intentions, was he happy? It wasn't enough for him to merely say he was happy, she needed to *feel* he was. Only then would her heart and spirit settle.

She let the words fill her up, *been busy... weather good... Big*

Reds are smashing it... looking forward to summer... I have news... are you sitting down?

'Oh! Oh Lord!' Vera read the words and received the news like a punch to the throat. It was unexpected and jarring. She re-read the lines as her heart rattled in her chest. 'Oh my!'

'You okay Vera?'

She hadn't heard Mira come in and felt the flame of embarrassment over her chest and neck. It felt a lot like being found out and she was more than a little flustered.

'I'm fine! Good morning, Mira, it's a beautiful day!' Jumping up so she stood straight, she did what she did best, dug out a wide smile and pulled her shoulders back.

'It is a beautiful day,' the girl nodded, her tone a little quiet, a little cautious, 'you look, you look a little sad,' the girl bit her lip, as if uncertain if it was the done thing to mention it.

'I just got a letter,' she waved the envelope in front of her face, stating the obvious, 'but I'm good. I'm good, sweetie.'

'Who's the letter from?' Mira asked casually, as she hung up her book bag on the peg by the back door.

'What do you think of my hair? I've already had one insult and one double-take and it's not even ten a.m.!'

She tried for diversion, not willing or able at that precise moment to talk about her son. Still careful to hide the detail of her life with him and right now, still digesting his news.

'I like it.' Mira pushed her tortoiseshell glasses up onto her nose and stared at Vera's head.

'Thank you! It was supposed to be subtle, but aint nothing subtle about it!'

She spoke loudly, slipping the letter into the pocket of her tunic and patting her curls while laughing. Experience had taught her that with enough laughing, enough joking, even the saddest of things could be doused in honey that made it a whole lot sweeter to swallow.

Mira hung her cardigan on top of her bag and went

straight to the tumble dryer to remove the towels. The two worked in a well-choreographed dance, each moving around the floor with precision, knowing instinctively when to reach for a towel, or magazine, when to make coffee or lemonade, when to move the dryer, check a permanent, mix bleach or offer a tissue, they kept one eye on their client in the chair and another on the clock. Timing was everything in a business like this. Too much or too little time and colours, tints, toners and treatments might fail. Timing was also vital to keep the well-oiled cogs of their appointment system turning in such a compact space. One client in, one client out, it was so slick that more often than not they would have a coat hanger in their hand where someone had retrieved a coat to leave when the next customer arrived, and that hanger would feel the weight of a new coat. Yes, it was a dance of sorts with the two of them comfortable in the steps. They stopped for lunch when they could, but rarely at the same time. One eating quickly, one watching both the clock and the door. Soup in the winter, salad in the summer, with the occasional flapjack or brownie to eat with their afternoon tea, usually a gift from a grateful regular. It worked.

'Who's first in the hot seat today?' Vera asked over her shoulder as she stood in the restroom and retouched her make up, applying the wand loaded with sparkly lilac eyeshadow over her lid and taking her time to perfect the cat's eye flick of liner that had been smudged a little by a rogue tear. Next and finally, she swiped the pink lip gloss over her pout and les voila! All restored. It was only anyone looking closely who would see the tremor to her hand and the wide pupils that belied her sunny disposition.

'Mrs Darby.' Mira read from the book.

'Ah, Verity, she's a nice lady and a good friend, could we ask for a better start to our day?' It was true, she looked forward to seeing Verity, reminding herself to mention that she'd seen Jack earlier.

'No ma'am, and then we have Barb McVey.'

'Great.' Vera popped on her apron and stared at her reflection, *Oh Knox! Knox!*

'I squeezed her in, she's coming right after she leaves the gym. She just wants a wash and blow out because Brian is taking her out for dinner. Then Greta Garbo's in to get her roots done and after that we've got Shrek in for a mani-pedi.'

'Perfect. Thank you, Mira.'

'I knew you weren't listening!' The girl laughed. 'Vera, you sure you're okay?'

'Sorry honey, a little distracted is all.'

'Because of your letter?'

Vera smiled wryly, the girl was sweet and itching to know who, why and where the letter was from, but when it came to her personal life, and especially her son, that was private. She had worked in salons before where gossip was currency and exchanging tittle-tattle was about as common as drinking tea, but not here, not in her salon. She was a woman of integrity who knew the value of keeping a still tongue, no matter how much the lack of information now irked young Mira.

Not that Linden Falls, for all its prettiness, was a town without secrets and gossip. Margot's illness for example, had been confided when a handful of her hair came away in the basin. Sworn to secrecy, Vera had told no one. And Verity Darby had come in for an up-do for the quiet, secret wedding to her beau Jack, that too she had not shared. And then there were those who asked for a favour – without the cash to pay for their daughter's prom hair, bridesmaids who declared the bride had the worst taste in the world and asked for revisions to their style. All of it Vera kept close to her chest, smiling widely, trying to please everyone and showing absolute respect to all. She, more than most understood the value of secrets and figured if she wanted hers kept, then it was only right she kept them for others.

'Something like that.' She washed her hands. The best reply she could muster. The sound of the little bell above the door tinkling, spared her further conversation and Mira, thankfully, bustled into action. It was Verity Darby.

'Good morning! Good morning! Hello darlings. Gosh, it's absolutely boiling out there already, going to have to dig out my linen frocks I think, not that I've bought new clothes for yonks. I seem to spend my life in dirty jeans! The life of a farm hand. A tired farm hand at that, I'm bloody knackered. Jack has a list of jobs as long as my arm and the place is like the Forth Bridge, you just finish one end and the other needs doing immediately. So many chores, who knew?'

The woman's British vowels and exuberant manner always made Vera smile. She liked listening to her accent and loved just as much that Verity had often said, 'I love your voice, Vera, could listen to you for hours…' She had always thought her own voice a little nasal and not in the least refined. It was a salient lesson that the appeal of a voice, or anything else for that matter, was entirely dependent on the person doing the judging. Verity had also confessed that in London she had her hair done by 'Nicky Clarke,' whoever that was, at a cost that seemed impossible to believe. Vera had whistled, 'I sure hope she was worth it! I'd want a lift home in a limo for that as well!'

'Are you okay, darling?' Verity placed her hand on Vera's arm, 'you look a bit…' the woman studied her face. That was all it took, this attention, this questioning coming from a place of love, of concern and Vera felt the awkward slip of tears over her cheeks,

'Now will you look at that, I don't know what's come over me!'

Grabbing a tissue from the box on the counter, she shoved it under her eyes, caring less about the racoon look but more embarrassed to be so distressed in front of Mira and Verity. No matter that the woman had long ago smudged the line between friend and customer.

It was no use, almost as if once her sadness found a route, she couldn't hold it back. Hot tears clogged her nose and throat, like someone had turned a tap on her distress.

'Oh darling! This isn't at all like you! Come on, let's walk.' Verity grabbed her bag and opened the door. 'Mira, I'm kidnapping Vera, back in a jiffy!'

'But... but I need to get you washed and trimmed,' she protested, aware of how messing up the timing this early on in the day could have disastrous results for the whole day. Like pushing one domino, which sat at the start of a long line.

'Forget about it, we can do hair any time. I'll reschedule, come on. This is not the time for hair trimming. We need fresh air and coffee! And possibly a doughnut. Maybe even two doughnuts!'

Vera caught the wink between Verity and Mira who waved and nodded her agreement that she'd hold the fort. It felt good to let someone else steer her, take the reins, care for her so openly.

The two women stepped out into the morning sunshine, walking slowly along the sidewalk as the residents of Linden Falls went about their business. It appeared to be a regular morning for everyone, except Vera, who had had her routine and her sensibilities entirely thrown. There was a line waiting outside the bank. The cluster of tables outside of the "Cobblestone Bakery" were mostly taken with men in khakis nursing coffee as they tip-tapped into their phones and women in sunglasses watching the world go by. Some had dainty pooches on leads, who sat quietly as their owners sipped chai latte and one or two sank their teeth into enviably plump croissant. Vera tipped her head back and took a deep breath.

'I'm sorry Verity, what must you think? I don't know

what's come over me.' She shook her head as those darned tears just kept on coming.

'Don't care about what I or anyone else thinks, that's the secret. And never apologize for your emotions. It happens sometimes.' Verity took her time, 'a few years back when my ex-husband had an affair, a very public affair that was humiliating, and something that changed my whole life,'

'And the reason you came to Linden Falls, all the way from London,' Vera filled in, everyone knew that the smart British lady had come on a vacation and never left, falling in love with Jack Darby and making her home a little way out of town in an old farmhouse with a view down over the valley.

'Yes,' Verity smiled as if the thought of meeting her Jack and that time in her life was only to be remembered fondly. 'I couldn't stop crying. I'd think I'd got it together and then pow! Out of nowhere the feeling would hit me in the chest, and I'd have to let it out. It felt a lot like grief. Still does sometimes even now when I'm living the most unimaginably wonderful life! But it can still overwhelm me, jab me when I least expect it.'

'That kind of sums it up.' Vera blew her nose into her tissue.

'The thing is it needs to come out sooner or later, and so you cry, you wail, you scream your lungs out and beat your fists if it makes you feel better.' Verity sat at one of the shady benches that edged the town square with a great view over the Linden Tree and Vera sat next to her. 'You know it'll go no further. You can talk to me darling.'

And just like that, Vera felt able to voice the twist of thoughts that snaked around her brain, wanting to share the storm of regret and recollection that swirled and jostled in her mind.

'I got a letter today, a letter from my son.'

Verity turned to face her. 'I didn't know you had a son.

How old is he?' Her tone wasn't shocked or judgemental and it helped oil the wheels of openness.

'He'll be twenty-seven this Christmas. Twenty-seven, doesn't seem possible.' She shook her head at this truth.

'And what's his name?' Verity asked, she was clearly interested and not simply asking for the sake of gossiping.

'His name is Knox.'

'Knox, as in Fort?' It sounded funny in her Queen's English.

'The very same.'

'It's not a name I know. Is it a name?'

'Yes!' Vera tutted. 'It's a name! There were two in my class in High School. I always kinda liked it.' Vera smiled to remember the nice boys who sat in her memory, 'they were polite, one wore shiny shoes and the other always had a decent bagged lunch,' she had no doubt it would have been made by an attentive momma who did not spend the day on a greasy chair surrounded by chaos.

'Really?' Verity stared at her, 'We had a handful of Benjamins, a few Williams, couple of Tristram's and a Rupert, but I don't recall a Knox.'

Vera knew her friend was trying to make her laugh and it worked. She smiled at the memory of holding her son in her arms, naming him, feeding him, kissing his little face, and knowing she would want nothing more for the rest of her days that to lie next to this tiny human and watch him sleep...

'Some folks know I have a boy, Neva for one, but I guess there's not many around here who keep secrets from Neva,' the woman who ran the B&B, Linden Falls very own "Curator of Wishes" was confidante to most in the community. 'I've heard all sorts of rumours doing the rounds. That my son's a bum, in jail, out of jail, an addict, and worse. I just smile politely and let the gossip reach a peak and exhaust itself, like any tornado, I figure it can only keep spinning for so long.'

'You're right of course. People can be cruel and jolly nosey. It's not a great combination. I remember some of the things that was said about me when my marriage broke up – funny how I recall some of the mean stuff and hardly any of the nice things people said.'

'Aint that the truth. The fact is I didn't grow up anywhere near as nice as Linden Falls. My parents were fond of reminding us that we couldn't buy a hummingbird on a string for a nickel.'

'Rightyo.' Verity nodded but Vera could tell she had no idea what she was talking about.

'I was always stick thin; the boys weren't interested in a skinny little thing like me, they wanted girls with bosoms,'

'I always had bosoms and envied the skinny girls.'

'We should have swapped places, Verity!'

'We should indeed! I'd have very much liked to have got to know the Knox with the good lunch.'

Both women laughed. Theirs was an easy camaraderie that today Vera welcomed.

'I never had much confidence, even though my momma used to say I had "good bones", and I'd ask her, which bones? And she'd reply, "All of 'em! Sharp cheek bones, and a strong back!" I knew what she meant. Working hard has always been second nature to me and with my sturdy elbows I was never afraid to sticking 'em out and getting stuck in. I saw the way my mom lived, and it made me determined to be nobody's fool. Especially when it came to men and money.'

'She sounds like a smart woman, took me bloody decades to figure that out.'

'Well, I stuck to my guns, didn't let anyone get too close, until I met Knox's dad and he,' she struggled to find the words, despite the easy exchange it was still hard to talk about Bill. 'He had something about him that made me open up. I loved him so much. I'd have done anything for him,' *apart from stay...* the words came unbidden and sent a tremor of sorrow right through her, 'but the one good thing to come out of it was Knox.'

'So, he lives with his dad?' Verity was curious, and Vera was confident that whatever they shared would not be tittle tattle to be shared over a maple creemee at The Soda Fountain, any time soon.

'Not initially, for the first decade it was just him and me. Oh, such happy times!' Again, she felt the hot creep of emotion at what came after. 'He went to live with his dad when he was thirteen and I could see he needed to be in that world and not in mine.'

'What world is that exactly?' Her friend asked softly.

'A world of smart people, of books and learning, academia. His dad's smart. Knox is smart too. It figures.' She shrugged, as if it was no big deal, which belied the dichotomy she had faced; giving him up for the life he deserved, whilst the knife of loss sat firmly lodged in her chest.

'Says you running your own business, skillfully making us all feel and look brilliant!'

She shook her head, 'no, I mean real smart.' Aware time was marching on and knowing there was too much to pass on in this one chat, she changed tack, 'anyway, I got a letter from Knox today telling me he's getting married, and that he's happy, so happy.'

'Well, I can see why you're so upset, who wants a happy, smart child with a lovely wedding on the horizon? No wonder you're utterly devastated.'

Again, Vera laughed.

'I'm glad he's getting married. But I'm upset because he's bringing her here.'

'Bringing who?' Verity asked with a wrinkle to her nose as if she'd lost the thread.

'His fiancé! His beautiful fiancé, Ashley who is also a professor,'

'Your son's a professor?'

'See!' She pointed at Verity, 'that's the look, the expression that says it all, *how can a woman like me have a son like that?* And I know it because that's what I think too! How can I? What do we have in common? What will Ashley think of me and what am I supposed to do, pull out the couch in my trailer for them?'

'You're wrong,' Verity shook her head, 'my expression is one of amazement *because* you have a son like that, and it would be the same whoever had a son like that! It's one hell of an achievement. Plus, in your build up you didn't mention it, but a professor, that's really something. If my daughter Sophia was a professor, it'd be the first thing I told anyone, like literally! It's marvellous.'

'I know it.' She smiled at her friend, 'I guess...' Her admission didn't come easy, 'I guess I don't want him to be ashamed of me, ashamed of all I haven't got, the life I don't lead.'

'He's your son! He won't care if you live in a skip or a castle!'

'What's a skip?' She hadn't heard the term.

'Oh, a dumpster – we call them skips.'

'Why?'

'I have no idea, Vera, but that's not what's we're discussing.' They both chuckled at the tangent. 'I'm quite sure they could care less if they sleep on your pull-out couch, but if you're worried about space or think it might be awkward, get them rooms at the Inn. Or I can even scrub up the cabins if you're desperate, get Jack to move his easels and paints for a weekend, it won't kill him.'

'Bless you Verity, thank you. I'm pretty sure Neva will have rooms or room, is probably more appropriate with them being engaged and all.'

Verity took her hand, and the contact warmed her; Vera couldn't remember the last time someone had comforted her in this way.

'You are a wonderful woman, a fabulous human! And it sounds to me like you made huge sacrifices for your boy,' Vera nodded, she sure had, 'and the fact that he is coming all the way out here with Ashley, excited for her to meet his mum says it all. He's rightly proud of you, it will all be fine. You'll see. I'll do whatever you need to help. That's what mates are for.'

'Thank you.' She squeezed the woman's arm. Her words had certainly eased the flustered thoughts, which rang around her head. 'I'd better get back to Mira.'

Slowly they made their way back to the salon before Verity promised to reschedule and squeezed her arm before leaving. Maybe Knox was proud of her in his own way, and it was good to know, but it was a whole other story when it came to being proud of herself and this, she knew, was the real issue.

'Good morning Barb,' she greeted the woman who had arrived a smidge before her and whose expression suggested she was more than a little displeased. 'Now isn't it just the most beautiful day?'

CHAPTER 3

*D*usk. It was Vera's favourite time of day when heat was replaced with the lilac bruise of twilight. A soft breeze whistled around the deck, grazing her bare skin with light relief from the sunshine, which both cooled her down and calmed her soul. Bugs came a buzzin', birds a chirpin' and all manner of Mother Nature's creations decided it was safe to come outside and take great lungfuls of the air as sweet as nectar, with promise of what tomorrow might bring... How she wished she shared their enthusiasm for what lay ahead, but nerves and self-doubt provided unpleasant filters when she considered Knox' proposed visit.

She finished her salad, drank a cold Diet Coke, and washed and put away her plate, cutlery, and drinking glass before wiping down the counter. Her busyness was only a means of putting off making the call, but without any other pressing chores, she took her time, knowing she wouldn't sleep a wink if she didn't find the courage. *Knox and Ashley... coming here...* this was her preoccupation. Along with another thought that thrilled and horrified her in equal measure, *Bill...* she would surely have to see him at the wedding.

The addition of this man into the mix did nothing to ease her concerns. What would it be like to see him again after all this time at their son's wedding? How long had it been? Nearly fifteen years give or take. Of course, it went without saying that he would be invited, and the thought only added another level of complexity to her dread. It wasn't so much about how she looked physically, although yes, she had aged, as had he of course, but was more about the person she had become, living alone, living quietly, going gently, working hard, and keeping her head down, what was it he used to say, *'you're a rocket V! You can shoot for the moon, reach the stars! You have that energy! You can do anything!'*

'Not sure about that.' She spoke aloud to no one that was listening and pictured the man who called her "V", who had stolen her heart and knocked her whole world sideways in the process.

Bill Morley had been the love of her life. *Her Billy...* they'd met one fall when she was waitressing at a diner in Ithaca, New York State, looking over one of the red brick Ivy League buildings and all within a short hop of the Finger Lakes.

It was a small, place with compact booths, a room-length counter and where notices and posters for clubs and gigs littered the door and walls. A place where cheap, hot food was served up by the bowlful to hungry students and faculty staff too lazy to cook, all looking for somewhere warm and homely to study. The diner fulfilled all these requirements. It was the 'in' place where coffee was on tap, eggs were expertly cooked and the toast was served piping hot, with just the right amount of butter.

Vera liked to be among it. Knowing she could never be part of it. Her, the girl who had failed to graduate high school, and yet she lived *in* it, saw this world up close, felt the weight of the heavy textbooks while she swept crumbs from tables. She picked up college-coloured scarves that had fallen from the backs of chairs, watched the scramble to get out of the door when the clock struck, and students rushed to get to class, and listened to the interaction of her customers across the tables while she lay down plates of crispy hash browns topped with the glossiest of salt sprinkled yolks,

'Have you read Dr Gale's text on the Eucharist debate?'

'Who hasn't? I found it a little assumptive...'

'Oh, you did? You need to read his essay on Transubstantiation V Consubstantiation, it's compelling.'

'But you're an atheist, surely?'

'Of course!' The boy had laughed, 'science, not science fiction!'

They didn't believe in God? She thought everyone believed in God, how in *God's name* could they not believe in God?

It was another world, and a world in which she moved quietly and anonymously like a ghost. Slipping and twirling between the kitchen, counter, and booths, plopping down bottles of ketchup and milkshakes in one of four flavours. Drinks so thick the straw stayed right where she put it in the middle of the glass. Yes, she was a ghost who spent her shift responding to clicked fingers, raised hands, waved menus or the bright ring of the bell above the door that heralded arrival. Canadian bacon on English muffins with French mustard – this dish made her smile; it was like she travelled all over God's green earth just by the food she placed in front of hungry students, who also came from all over! Not that she engaged with them, she was after all invisible to them, but to see texts in alphabets that looked like something from another planet – it fascinated her. Equally it made her feel stupid.

She had always been aware of her lack of book learning, but seeing this world close up showed her just how much she didn't know, and it was a lot. She'd never heard of Dr Gale; didn't know how or why you'd read someone else's essay. And as for those squiggly lines and all them dots and dashes, what language was it? Looked like something you might find in ancient Egypt! But how could anyone read *that*?

Vera had loved her job. She worked hard, smiled a lot, and gathered up nickels and dimes to pop into her savings jar, which grew heavier by the day. All the while, unbeknown to her, Billy was close by, hoovering up knowledge, devouring weighty books with pancakes and cherry compote as a side order. Then one ordinary, unremarkable night, as she stood behind the counter, popping coins into little plastic bags ready to be shipped to the bank the next morning, topping off the mugs of a couple of sobering stragglers with stewed coffee, and with feet throbbing inside her sneakers, she walked over to his table with the check. And her night, indeed her whole world, was in an instant, made extraordinary and quite remarkable.

The man looked up and she looked down and there was a moment the like of which she hadn't experienced before or since, but it was a moment that she would never forget and one that replayed in her head like a scene from a movie on more days than she would ever admit. She often wondered if she'd imagined it or embellished it, but forensic and frequent dissection of the memory told her this was not the case.

How best could she describe it? Like a lightning bolt. Yes, that was it, like a lightning bolt that struck her heart and in some way that was a mystery to her, joined her to the man who looked up through his glasses and smiled. He wasn't local, his accent gave that away; she had seen him before maybe once or twice but hadn't really *seen* him… he was one of those people, like so many, who flew under the visual radar. Just another student with his nose in a book, his left hand flicking the pages, following text with his forefinger while with his right, he used the edge of the fork to break up his omelette and feed his mouth, pausing only momentarily to drop the fork, pick up a pen and annotate a page or circle some text. They all did this; all of her customers, unable to take a break from the world of learning that held them fast, even to eat! She was as fascinated by the process as she was by the people themselves. He didn't wear elaborate or extravagant clothes, no bright colours, bold hat or anything that made him stand out. His hair was brown, his eyes brown, his shoes brown, his jacket brown, his height average, build medium and a voice that wasn't overly loud or soft. Yet in that moment when she stood at the table, and he looked up and took off his glasses, her eyes fixed in a stare as she studied him, and the first thing she noticed was his eyes; liquid pools into which she dived. Mind body and soul she tumbled – entirely lost to anything he might say or do. To her in that moment and every moment since, he stood out as something bright and beautiful, as if the whole wide world and everything in it were flat and he the only thing that was three dimensional. The way he made her feel was extraordinary too. So, what *did* he say? What was the phrase that fired the thunderbolt, lancing her reserve and setting her heart on a path from which there would be no emotional deviation? The exchange was etched perfectly in her memory.

'Bill, it's Bill.'

That's what he said. That's all he said and that was all it took.

'Huh?' She felt the blush of embarrassment to have lost the thread so early in the conversation.

'Did… did you ask me my name?' He stuttered, his eyes never leaving hers.

'I did not.'

'Oh.' He sat back in the chair with an air of disappointment that was strangely elating, as if he hoped she had asked. His kind eyes crinkled, and she noted his full bottom lip that was attractive.

'Vera.' She smiled, 'that's me.'

'That's you.' He beamed. 'Vera.'

'I haven't seen you here before.' She lied, not knowing, as nerves coated her tongue, how to continue the conversation without lying.

'I've been in once or twice. I stay across the road above the laundromat in a shared house.' He pointed. 'It can get a bit noisy, a bit crazy, lots of big personalities. So, I come here, read, eat… peace and quiet.' He placed his hand on his open textbook and she took in his clean, neat nails. Fingernails of a man who would earn his money with his head and not his hands. It made her think of her brothers and their many battle scars.

'Student?'

'Yes, Cornell, obviously,' he plucked at the scarf on the table, 'studying for my PhD.'

'What're you studying?'

'I'm a scientist, biomedics.'

'Right.' She flipped the paper check back and forth over her fingers, didn't want to end their conversation but was aware of the need to clean down, lock up, throw out the last of the coffee, catch the bus. And with zero idea of what "*biomedics…*" might mean.

'Are you a student too?' He broke her train of thought.

'Me? A student?' She had hollered her laughter with her hand on her chest, 'no! No, I'm not.' But the fact that he didn't match her laughter and had, in all seriousness, posed the question, made her feel like a million dollars. He always did, that was his trick…

VERA SLUNK back on the sofa cushion, curled her legs beneath her and lifted her phone. It was crazy, but she pressed the number and closed her eyes, hoping, praying at some level he wouldn't answer, feeling nervous about what to say if he did, where to begin…

'Mom!'

The sound of his voice enough to erase some of her nerves, his eager and happy tone, even more so.

'Hey darlin' how are you?'

'Good, good, did you get my letter?' He sounded excited and young.

'I sure did.' She looked at the envelope propped up on the mantelpiece and her heart skipped. 'That's partly why I'm callin' to say, congratulations! I can't believe it; my son is getting married! How is that even possible? One minute you're waddling around in diapers and the next choosing a tux!'

'I can't believe it either, although I don't think it'll be a tux kind of wedding. More board shorts and beer if I get my way.'

'And what about Ashley, is that her vision for her special day?' It felt odd, discussing the girl she couldn't pick out in a line up and yet who was going to be her daughter-in-law. Knox laughed, as if at the absurdity of his own suggestion.

'Not quite!' He drew a slow breath, 'we're still ironing out the details, and I know it's real quick, but I remember you saying to me years ago, when you know you know, and I know!'

'Well, I think Ashley is very lucky.' This she meant.

'I'm the lucky one mom, she's… she's so great.'

His tone of affection warmed her heart. 'I want all the details! Are you happy? Of course, you're happy! Stupid question! Where d'you meet?'

'At Cornell, she was a guest lecturer and for the twelve weeks she was on campus, I have never been so interested in Oceanography.'

She laughed along with him, but it was just this kind of topic that sent a bolt of inadequacy right through her. College professors, that was their job and subjects like nanomedicine, her son's specialism, and oceanography were as familiar to him as the bleach and toners she handled daily. It was another world.

What was it Bill had always said? *"If you don't like the world you are in, build a better one..."* It made her smile.

'And you've met her people?'

'Her people?'

Did she detect humour in his question, was he laughing at her? It was amazing how quickly the hammer of doubt came down to crush any kernel of confidence that dared show itself.

'Yes, yes Mom and you are going to love them! I know it.' And just like that she cursed the questioning of her son's tone, his words sweet, excited, and inclusive, 'they live in Syracuse, so we see them quite often, only a car ride away – I know you'll like them. I've told them all about you,'

'Not that much to tell.' She cut in. He either didn't hear or didn't acknowledge it.

'Her mom Miko is sweet, and her dad Andrew, a wannabee sailor who loves the water. They have a boat.'

Andrew with a boat? Vera wondered how much or how little she might have in common with him.

'That sounds great. Really great, and what can I do to help with the wedding, how are plans coming along?'

'Ash's parents are quite old fashioned and have been saving for her big day pretty much since she was born,'

Oh God! *Quite old fashioned*, what would they make of the fact that she and Bill had never married, and she'd raised Knox alone until he was thirteen? Would they understand that Knox had extraordinary potential and that Bill, as his smart dad, was the man to help him lead his very best life... No matter that it split her heart in two on the day she waved him off and that was how it had stayed with a splinter of loss lodged right there in the middle. Knowing that each day he lived Bill's life was a day that took him further and further away from her. On the road of life, Bill, wrapped up in academia with his smart, bookish friends, dusty antiques and traveling to look at ruins - was at one end of the line and she, in her trailer with her little business and a closet full of denim and sequins was at the other.

'I'll let her tell you all about it, I think we're arriving on Thursday early evening, and we'll only be with you til Sunday afternoon, but enough time for you guys to meet,'

'You're, you're coming here next week?'

She felt her mouth go dry at the prospect and looked around her pretty home wondering how she was going to accommodate guests with only one small couch – would they sit outside and stare at Mrs Kenny, topping and tailing her string beans? She knew they were coming at some point, but *next week*? This left no time to plan, no time to make alterations, but just enough time to panic. She did her best to control the jump in the rhythm of her breathing, not wanting to give her beloved son the tiniest of inklings that he and his fiancé's impending arrival was not the very best thing imaginable. Which it was of course, if only they'd stay elsewhere.

'Did you not get my voicemail? I left you a message earlier. Yes, we're coming next week!'

She recalled a small flashing light on her screen, so *that's* what it meant...

'Sorry honey, me, and technology! That'll be wonderful! I can't wait to see you and to meet Ashley.'

'Well, I figured, as I've asked you often enough to come to Ithaca and I know you don't like to travel, I thought this would be easier. Us coming to you.'

Vera closed her eyes, knowing she had indeed said that she didn't like to travel, it wasn't strictly true, she didn't mind the idea of seeing new places and even revisiting the old, but the last thing she wanted to do was run into Bill. But this was happening, Knox and Ashley were coming here to Linden Falls. Her pulse raced.

'I can't wait for you to meet her, Mom.'

His tone suggested he wanted her approval and whilst as a grown man, he of course did not need anyone's permission to follow his heart, it felt nice to know it was important to him.

'And I can't wait to meet her.' This was, all her doubts aside, the truth, she smiled and held the phone close to her face.

'I was just thinking, you guys might like to stay up at "White Cedar Farm", owned by friends of mine, Verity and Jack. They have a couple of beautiful cabins with the prettiest views down over the valley.'

'They sound great, but I'd prefer to stay with you. I know Dad will love being on a farm though, he still rolls up his sleeve and fully commits to the role whenever he gets near a field.'

His words were like hot knives through her throat, and she felt the tremble to her limbs. 'Your... your dad?'

She knew it was inevitable their path's would cross at the wedding, but *next week?* Her heart raced.

'Yes, I mean of course Dad's coming. I didn't want the first-time you guys saw each other again after all this time to be at the wedding, how awkward would that be? I thought it was a good idea to all get together before. Break the ice.'

'Great,' she did her best to control the tremor to her voice, 'it's a great idea!'

'Are you doing what you do, Mom? Saying it's great but secretly digging your nails into your palms and tensing your jaw?'

She unclenched her fingers and wiggled her mouth to loosen the muscles.

'No, not at all! I think you're right; we don't want to add any more pressure to your wedding day, not that it's about me and your dad, it's all about you guys. It will be good to see him.'

Having said her good-byes, she immediately called Verity.

'Hello darling, how're you doing? I've been worried about you all day; you were jolly upset earlier.'

'I'm good. Thank you for being there for me, not my finest hour.'

'I'll always be there for you! As I said, that's what mates do.'

'Well, it meant a lot, Verity. And I need to ask, when you offered to scrub up your cabins for Knox and Ashley, did you really mean it?'

Vera closed her eyes and waited for her friend to reply.

CHAPTER 4

*I*t was Thursday evening. Vera had let Mira style her hair and not done a bad job. Cassie from Claudine's Bistro had dropped her in some fresh asparagus, greens and radishes picked straight from her garden and which now graced the small table in Verity's kitchen, as Vera paced the deck with a twitch to her fingers. Not that she had much of an appetite. She was nervous, no, beyond nervous, a wreck! For the seventh time in an hour, she straightened the collar of her shirt and ran her hand over the pink braided belt that held up her jeans. It had taken her an age to decide what to wear, shorts felt too informal, too revealing. Her summer dresses, like she was trying too hard. So, jeans it was, neat jeans, teamed with a crisp cotton, floral blouse, and her hair, the colour toned down to a plum/brunette, swept up on top in a way that Mira had perfected. She felt the surge of nervous energy in her gut.

'You okay Vera?' Jack asked in the languid manner that was his trademark, as he walked from the field back into the house, a cardboard box in his hand, full of what she dared not ask.

'Bit nervous.'

'Don't be. Remember people all feel the same, and if you're nervous, they probably are too. It's quite a thing to meet your future ma-in-law. Heck, I was scared half to death of my future stepdaughter, her dad, his new wife...' He blew out his cheeks at the memory, he knew just how to lighten the moment. 'I guess the fact is, life gets complicated as you get older and it's all about making space in your lives for people you didn't know you had to make space for, but it all kinda works out in the end if it's meant to.'

'Well, it did for you.'

She smiled at the man. He and Verity were serenely happy, contentment shaped their every word and action. She thanked God for the state her friends lived in and prayed that she might one day be half as lucky.

'It did.' He nodded. 'We've got your back.'

'Thanks Jack.' His words meant the world.

With the sun still shining in the late afternoon sky, she took a moment to breathe deeply, to calm her flustered pulse and try and erase the tangle of fraught emotions that filled her mind. She was scared and her hands shook accordingly. It was as she opened her eyes that she heard the whine of an engine and saw the plume of dust, kicked up by wheels on the rutted track. From the deck, she saw the car make its way along the lane.

'They're here!' She called back into the house, partly as excitement meant the words sprang from her and partly because she wanted Verity, at least, to be in close proximity.

'Oh fab!' Verity came and stood on the step, a little way behind her, but Vera was no less glad of her presence. 'This is exciting!'

Knox! Vera felt the familiar rise of emotion in her throat. It was always this way, to see him, hear him, read his words in a letter, any contact at all and it was like taking the plug out of a pot and all that she managed to keep pent up and hidden away came pouring out. She waved at the man with the chestnut-coloured hair in the front seat. Her son! Her son, the newly appointed professor, and more jarring, a full-grown man.

Ridiculously, this was always a surprise to her, as if she expected him to remain the teenager who used to sit opposite her at the little table in their old apartment, sitting on the rickety chair under the buzzing strip light, dipping Graham Crackers into a jar of Cheez Whiz and sharing snippets about his day that would leave her bamboozled. Puzzling over math equations and reading books on the human body while she watered her plants and shouted out the answers to the questions Alex Trebek asked through her TV screen. And now here he was, a handsome man, all grown up. She guessed it would always feel this way, unbridled joy at the sight of him, bookended with immeasurable sorrow for all she had missed, for every day on God's earth she spent without sight of the human she had grown and birthed.

He raised his hand, before pointing to her, and a young woman in the back seat leaned forward to look. *Ashley...* The girl was beaming, her smile open, her long dark hair cascading around her shoulders, eyes wide in excitement and she was... she was so beautiful! There was only the cab driver, no Bill. This she noted with a mixture of extreme relief and intense disappointment, having psyched herself up for the reunion and taken extra care to iron her blouse and apply just the right amount of scent.

'Are you okay sweetie?'

The voice behind her almost made her jump, she'd forgotten that Verity, her wingman was behind her.

'I'm good.' She smiled at her friend.

'Mom!'

And just like that, there he was, walking briskly towards her, half running, and oh, oh to feel his arms around her, holding her close. It was a feeling that came to her in dreams, the contact with this person who would always be connected to her, this person who owned her whole heart. Holding him close, the feel of the child she dreamed of, solid beneath her fingertips, it was pure joy! It was with reluctance she had to let him go, wanting to hold him forever.

'It's been a long time!'

She'd forgotten his easy manner, his knack of conversation, his calming nature, and his striking resemblance to his father, more so now that age put him close to the point when she had met Bill and her whole world, and everything she thought she knew had been turned upside down.

'Too long.' She managed through a mouth being pulled down with tears that gathered in her nose and throat.

'What a place! This is beautiful!' He let his arm move in a wide arc to indicate the surroundings and the incredible view down the valley.

'Well, this is Mr and Mrs Darby's place: Verity and Jack.'

'Welcome, welcome!' Verity clapped, 'is it just the two of you?' Vera had fully briefed her friend on the state of play when it came to Bill and the nerves that engulfed her.

'For now, yes. Dad came in on a different flight this morning, he's got a hire car, been exploring no doubt, and should be here any time. He likes to do his own thing.'

'Well thank goodness for that, thought I'd scrubbed the old cabin for nothing!'

Vera was grateful to her friend for asking, knowing she would be doing so to get the lie of the land for her mate.

'Thank you for inviting us, this really is something.' Knox addressed Jack with such reverence it made Vera's heart swell with pride.

'No problem, you like fishing?'

'Jack!' Verity batted at him, 'this is no time to talk about fishing!'

'Oh, with all due respect ma'am, I think any time is a good time to talk about fishing!' Knox fired back and Jack smiled approvingly at the boy. 'I do sir, not that I've got much time for anything right now.' He spoke from the side of his mouth, 'I had no idea how much detail and how many decisions go into a wedding. Every day it's something different; being asked to choose between this flower or that flower, and apparently, "I don't mind" is not the correct response. Dark or pale blue ribbon, buttercream, or Swiss meringue? It's another world!' He shook his head, conspiratorially but the smile to his eyes suggested the joy he actually felt at the whole carry on. 'Here she is.'

They all turned to watch Ashley step from the car, tucking her long, dark hair behind her ears, her shoulders a little dropped, hands clasped in front of her as if nervous or in reverence, both of which Vera understood. And in that moment, she felt a wave of empathy for the girl who was about to face three strangers in this new place.

A memory came to her of walking up the street on Bill's arm, off to meet his parents in the faculty restaurant for lunch with her heart pounding and her tongue stuck to the dry roof of her mouth.

'And so, what's the plan?' Bill's pointy nosed mother had asked as they sipped soup from deep spoons and Vera had concentrated on not slurping.

'The plan?' She had felt confused.

'Yes, William said you were working in a diner as a *temporary* measure...' The woman's sneer confirmed that this was a most unsatisfactory state of affairs.

Vera had shot Bill a look and he had shrugged, only confirming later at the height of their row that he had never used the word *temporary* and that its insertion was simply his mother trying to cause trouble, which, if the scale of their row was anything to go by, she had more than succeeded. The irony wasn't lost on Vera that in the wake of their argument, it had been during heated make-up sex that Knox had been conceived and that, it transpired, was the plan, to get knocked up and become a mom. Not that this was how she would have phrased it to "William's" mother, exactly.

Knox hurried over to the car, making sure his fiancé wasn't walking alone, an act so kind and supportive it sent a hard ball of emotion to lodge in Vera's throat. He put his arm across her back, gently guiding, steering in a way that spoke of tenderness that was both moving and enviable. There was no doubt that in this regard too, he took after his daddy. Bill had always been kind and tactile. This an unwelcome thought when she was doing her very best to keep everything together and not give in to the desire to howl her distress right there and then at how much she missed him every single day they were apart.

The girl was smiley, her face so pretty without a scrap of make-up, her skin olive but most striking was her open expression. Wide eyed, a little overwhelmed, sure, but a face that invited trust, invited love. Vera felt the knot in the base of her gut unwind a little.

'Hi.' Ashley bunched her fingers, as she climbed the wide steps up onto the deck, loosely addressing everyone.

'This is my mom.' He indicated, as Ashley stepped forward.

'I'm not sure what to call you?' She approached slowly and stood close, as if mutual scrutiny did not faze her. Confident.

'Oh, Vera will do fine. I answer to most things.'

'Hello Vera.'

'Hi Ashley.' It was almost instinctive, Vera reached for her hands and held them both, 'welcome to Linden Falls.'

'It's so beautiful.'

She watched as her future daughter-in-law's eyes took in the wide sweep of the valley along the ridge, the tall trees, clustered in forest that ran all the way down to the lake, yes, it was beautiful.

'I've been so nervous.' Ashley admitted and Vera liked her even more. She let go of her hands.

'*You've* been nervous!' Vera chuckled. 'I couldn't eat my breakfast! Which for me is quite a thing.'

'Well, it must be strange for you, Knox turning up with a future wife. It's a lot! I mean it's a lot for me, becoming a wife so it must be a lot for you too!'

'It is honey, but all I want, all I ever wanted, is for him to be happy and you seem like the person to do that. I mean look at you both!' She exchanged a glance with Verity who nodded her agreement, 'grinning like possums eating sweet tater!'

Ashley laughed loudly and Knox joined her.

'I'll go grab the bags from the trunk.' Knox ran back to the cab.

'I'll go make some tea.' Verity chimed.

'Oh, you're English!' Ashley noted.

'Guilty as charged.' Verity smiled at the girl.

'Whereabouts are you from?' Ashley asked with the assured tone of someone who didn't let nerves rattle them.

'London.'

'Oh, I love it! One of my favourite cities. We always stay near Hyde Park and walk everywhere!' Ashley was, she knew being chatty, showing kindness for Verity's homeland, but the fact that she had been to London, *knew* London, made Vera aware of her humble life, her small life where travel to another state had always felt like a big deal.

'Well, we were just off the Kings Road,'

'You're kidding! The Bluebird Café is one of my favourites!' Ashley practically danced on the spot.

'I know it very well.' Verity gave Vera a subtle wink, an expression of camaraderie, of sisterhood.

'Are you a Londoner too?' She asked Jack who leaned on the porch.

'Good God no!' He pulled a face that made them all laugh.

'Here we go.' Knox dumped the bags on the floor, 'I'll put the bags in your truck Mom.'

'Oh well, no, don't do that. I've arranged for you to stay in the cabins that Verity and Jack have right here on the farm, the ones I mentioned. You'd have passed them as you came in on the lane. They've got a lovely view, a deck, real pretty,'

He shook his head, 'that's really kind, but I'd rather we came to stay with you. We're only here for two full days and so it'll be good to spend it together. It's very kind of Mr and Mrs Darby,' he spoke loud enough for her friends to hear, 'but if we're all the way out here,'

'I… I don't have that much space,' she faltered, feeling her heart race at the prospect.

'We don't need much space, a couch is fine, a blow-up mattress on the floor, great! Whatever.'

'I guess,' she tried to swallow the rising tide of panic, 'I guess I could see if there are any rooms at the B&B that's no more than a quick walk to my place, it'd be closer…'

There was no mistaking the flash of hurt in his eyes and it killed her. How was she to explain that her home was no fit place for a professor, no, two professors! It wasn't that she didn't want him close, she did, but the cloak of shame that she'd been wearing since she was a child weighted her down and robbed her of her self-esteem.

'No that's fine.' His voice sounded a little clipped, 'if you really are that against us coming to stay with you then here will be just fine,'

'I'm not *against* it, Knox, it's just from a practical stand-point,' she interrupted.

'No that's fine, don't worry about it.' It was his turn to cut her short, 'we'll stay here. At least we're near Dad.' There was no mistaking his slight barb, 'when he turns up that is.'

'He still a little unsure when it comes to navigation?' She smiled weakly, trying to lighten the mood and restore the air of jollity that had prevailed only minutes before.

With perfect timing, a car beeped its horn that drew them all,

'I'd say he's managed to find us.'

Vera felt a little dreamlike, her legs had turned to Jell-o. She had, in the intervening years, often tried to imagine reunion between her and Bill, but it was difficult. Sure, the couple spoke on the phone from time to time, they did after all share their glorious boy, but visits to her son and his visits to her were always carefully crafted, arranged to happen in a place half way between them, and apart from rudimentary telephone discussions, avoided the inclusion of Bill. It was self-preservation of sorts.

All thoughts of him were trapped behind a filter that was nearly thirty years old, capturing him as he was a long time ago, and her too, like looking at a black and white cine film that took her right back to that time and place long gone. Any imaginings of reunion were in her mind only a poor imitation of the day they had met and how they had quickly and gloriously fallen in love. Not that she was foolish enough to believe it would be like that again, of course not, this was real life not some movie! But she'd be lying if she didn't admit that the thought of seeing him again sent a frisson of excitement through her very core. Bill was that person, the one who had got away and it had always felt like they had unfinished business.

The day she'd helped Knox pack his suitcase and load it into the back of her truck, before driving across states to deliver him safely to the man who she knew would develop his talent, steer him right, was one that lived with her. Never would she forget what it felt like to tamp down the loss that threatened to drown her and smile sweetly, as Bill, older yet still handsome, had greeted her with an easy smile and no murmur of nerves or anxiety. His manner only confirming that her decision was the right one.

'Coffee V? That must have been some journey.' He'd

spoken as if they'd only seen each other days before, like it was any casual visit and not with the intervening hiatus of a decade dividing their lives.

And now here he was.

It was all she could do not to stare at him, taking in every small detail.

He parked the car, opened the door, and swung his legs out. Aware of him, the shape of him, she noted the space he took up in the world because it was a space he took up in her mind and had for the longest time, since the day they had first met,

'Bill, it's Bill.'

'Huh?'

'Did... did you ask me my name?'

He looked broader, more padded than the last time she'd seen him, still tall, obviously, and his thick hair had touches of grey at the temples, but the years had been kind. The leap in her gut, the desire to be close to him, the feeling of unravelling in his presence as if he might know her thoughts, well, that was just the same. Acutely aware of all about her that had aged, sagged, and withered somewhat, she felt the tremble of anxiety as she waited for him to acknowledge her. When he did, it was to greet her with that wide and easy smile that she had captured perfectly, seeing it in her mind's eye before she fell asleep each night and was there to taunt her when she woke each morning.

'Well, there she is.' His words simple and yet groaning with meaning, as if he had been waiting for her, as if he too felt the powerful connection.

'Here I am!' She raised her hands, easy, as ever to smile, laugh, jest and smooth away the ripples of low self-esteem and nerves that threatened to topple her.

Walking forward, his stride purposeful, he took her by the tops of the arms and studied her face. The physical contact was... was... unnerving and electrifying in equal measure. Vera blinked, her desire to cry was strong but she swallowed that. This was no time for tears or regret, this was a sweet reunion, a happy time!

'I don't know about you young Ms Delaney but having a son old enough to get married makes me feel quite old.'

'Well, I've been feeling old for some time so it's nothing new to me,' she gave a tight smile, 'and I haven't been *young* Ms Delaney for a long time.'

'Of course!'

He let go of her arms and there was the gossamer like touch over her skin, a veil of embarrassment that wrapped them both. She knew Bill was not a vindictive man, didn't have a bad bone in his body, which could only mean one thing. He had forgotten why the association with her family name would cut her to the quick and if he truly had forgotten that, then it meant she had not lived in his mind, as he had hers. Maybe for him she was not a spring bloom that lie dormant for much of the time, but without warning would fill her thoughts with colour and form so bright it was all she could see, until it calmed and quieted again.

'It is so good to see you, V. So good.'

To hear her name on his lips was enough to unlock the words he had spoken through a mouth riven with tears and distress. What was the last thing he'd said to her on that day, when with Knox buckled up in the carry seat, she'd put her key in the ignition and prepared to drive away,

V... you're being crazy! You want to throw away our whole life because of how you think I might feel in the future? Vera please.... Please don't do this to us... get out of the car, come on, come back inside...

'It's good to see you too.' It was the truth.

'Hey Pop!' Ashley's greeting to her future father-in-law was a moment of clarity. It spoke of a closeness Vera could only imagine and feelings of exclusion rose in her gut.

'Aint this something,' he kissed the girl on the cheek and

stepped forward to shake hands with first Verity then Jack. 'I'm grateful of the invite, although be warned, I'm already thinking about staying here for good.'

Everyone laughed, except Verity, who exchanged a knowing look with Vera, and it was one of understanding, as if she knew enough to figure that this might not be a bad thing.

'I could sure do with the extra pair of hands.' Jack smiled. 'Plus, you better be warned my friend, we have a wishing tree, so be careful with those words!'

'Ha!' Bill laughed loudly, 'yes, I read about it, love any folklore tales! A wishing tree, now wouldn't that be something.'

'Tea! Tea in the kitchen with homemade carrot cake – my own recipe.' Verity halted the topic, diverting everyone, as the troupe now made their way into their beautiful farmhouse interior, where baskets of soft blankets sat next to linen toned sofas and the walls were of the palest shade of grey.

'This place is so gorgeous!' Ashley too took in the elegant décor and Vera, not for the first time wondered what the girl might make of Miss Emilia-Jane, Miss Jannette and their porcelain faced sisters...

With tea drunk, cake consumed and much laughter flowing back and forth between them all, Vera felt the most relaxed she had all day. Time was marching on, and she was aware of not over-imposing on their generous hosts.

'I should be getting on home and I'm sure Verity and Jack could do without us all cluttering up their kitchen!' She stood.

'So, what's the plan Mom?' Knox stood too and walked around the table to put his arm about her shoulders as he spoke. It was an act of forgiveness and placation, smoothing over their earlier sharp exchange, 'shall we come over to you in the morning?'

'Sure!' She found a smile, 'how about we meet in the town square, give Ashley a guided tour? I'm sure she'd like to see the famous Wishing Tree?'

'I would, but it's a joke, right? Like Punxsutawney Phil – a nice tale but not real!' She looked around the table.

'Depends on who you ask.' Verity nodded sagely.

'I'll drive us in. Now,' Bill stood and placed his napkin on the plate next to carrot cake crumbs, 'where is this cabin?'

'Well, Vera can show you all. She's driving out that way anyway, is that okay?' Her friend she noted, avoided eye contact.

'Sure. Just follow me!' She hollered. 'And thank you, Verity, Jack for everything, for making today so special.' She meant it. The Darby's had gone above and beyond.

'It's been our absolute pleasure!' Verity beamed, 'let us know if you need anything.'

'Call you later.' Vera locked eyes with her friend, knowing they would debrief and swap notes over the phone.

With their luggage stowed in Bill's hire car, Knox jumped into her truck for the journey along the lane, as Ashley rode with Bill.

'What do you think of her?' His question immediate, his tone a little anxious.

'I think she's beautiful, Knox. Beautiful inside and out.'

'I know right? I'm so lucky.' He swallowed suggesting this was an emotional time for him too.

'You both are,' it was second nature for her to try and remind him of his value, his gifts. 'Your Dad looks well.'

'I want him to be happy.' Knox looked over his shoulder and waved at the car behind, which Bill drove.

'You don't think he's happy?' This news she met with a frisson of expectation, because if Bill wasn't happy…

'I think he is in some respects, his career and whatever, but I don't want him to be lonely. I've told him this already.'

'So, what's the solution?' She was keen, as someone who understood loneliness to hear her son's words.

'The solution is for him to make the jump. Grab the reigns. Steer his own ship. Go for it! And not to let the years slip by... I am forever introducing him to anyone I think might be suitable, currently, I'm trying to arrange a dinner date with Melissa who works in the admin department.'

'And how's that going?' It surprised her how much she hoped the answer would be 'not that well.'

'Well, he's being cagey. He's yet to make a date stick, both are busy, I know that, but how hard is it to grab a coffee? I don't hold out much hope!' He laughed.

'You sound wise beyond your years Knox.'

'I guess I grew up quick when you gave me to Dad.' His words tumbled, like rocks that fell onto her chest.

A sharp breath caught in her throat, 'Gave you to Dad?' She let out a strangled laugh borne from acute discomfort. 'What a thing to say to me, Knox! I didn't give you to Dad! I didn't give you away! I let you go live with him, took you to go live with him, so you would have choices. Choices Knox! That's the ultimate good life, to be able to choose your path, choose your life! I didn't want you to have to put in shifts at the Piggly Wiggly and save up dimes for gas, I let you go and live with him so you could earn a living with your head not your hands, so you'd never know the throb of your feet when only halfway through a shift. So you could learn his study habits, mix with his friends, speak nice, afford to get sick, and get to a good college so that your life would be all that you deserved it to be. And you did, and you have!'

'So, I should thank you?' He held her gaze.

'Where is this coming from?' She turned to face him as she pulled up outside the front of the cabin.

'I guess,' Knox ran his palm over his face, 'I guess I've been thinking about things a lot, the way Ashley loves me makes me think about things and,' he paused.

'And what?' She pushed, hating the crack to her voice.

'And I feel strongly that you are keeping me at arm's length, and I've felt that way for the longest time. We can't stay in your home; we're meeting in town tomorrow…'

'Maybe it's more about not disappointing you than keeping you at arm's length.' She tried to explain.

'Disappointing me? You just don't get it do you?' His voice was raised a little now.

'So, tell me!' She wanted this conversation, wanted to understand how he felt about her and what the years had been like while in his daddy's care.

They were interrupted by Ashley appearing at the passenger window and pulling a funny face.

'She's always goofing around.' He held up his hand and Ashley placed hers on the other side of the glass. It was an act so intimate it almost felt intrusive to watch.

'Verity said the keys are under the mat.' Ashley ran up towards the cabin, as Vera wound down the windows.

'I guess I'll see you tomorrow, Mom.' He turned to face her, his expression hard to fathom, but certainly regretful.

'Yes, I'll see you tomorrow, son.' She whispered.

'You not coming in for a look around?' Bill hauled his weekend bag over his shoulder and stood by the side of her truck.

'No, think I'll call it a night. It's been good to see you, Bill.'

'It's been good to see you.' He waved as if in goodbye but didn't move.

'Do you think,' she began, her words jumping on her tongue enough to confuse a head already muddled with emotion.

'Do I think what?' He took a step closer, and she could inhale the scent of him, the savoury, masculine smell that was just as she'd remembered it. A smell that took her back decades to a time before she had "given her son away,"

'Do you think kids can ever understand the choices their parents make?'

'Wow, kind of deep and not what I was expecting, but,' he shifted the bag slightly as if the weight on his shoulder bothered his ageing bones, 'and I can only speak from my own experience, I think a lot of the things my folks did and said only gained clarity when I became a parent. I realised that a lot of what I thought was nagging was only them trying to keep me safe, and that many of their words were voiced through fear of the *what if?* I also believe there are only two ways to parent: we either learn from what our parents did, and we do the same. Or we learn from what our parents did, and we do different.'

'Aint that the truth.'

She felt her shoulders slump with the weight of her son's earlier sleight and watched as he and Ashley retrieved the key from the under the mat and run like excited kids into the cabin. The weight of Bill's stare was felt even though she looked away from him.

'You're still gorgeous V. You really are.'

His words caught her off guard and she did what she did best, waved a hand, snorted her laughter, and turned the compliment into a thing of awkwardness.

'You got your glasses on Mister?' She squinted up at him through the window.

'I'll see you tomorrow.' He patted the roof of her truck and she felt dismissed.

'You will indeed.'

Vera watched the man grow smaller in her rear-view mirror, and not for the first time she drove away from he and Knox, with a heart that groaned with all it tried to contain and feeling like an outsider.

CHAPTER 5

*V*era woke early, watered the plants on the porch, waved to Mrs Kenny and texted Mira her thanks for holding the fort in the salon today, with a reminder that she was only around the corner for any and all emergencies. Having positioned her dolls against the plump pillows, she sipped a glass of water and tried to rehearse all the things she wanted to say to Knox. His uncharacteristic snipe had left her reeling. *"Gave me away..."* She had replayed not only *what* he'd said, but also *how* he'd said it until the early hours. It had unsettled her in the way that only a comment like this from someone you loved, could.

Her phone rang. It startled her.

'Verity!'

'The green pig has left the barn. I repeat the green pig has left the barn.'

'What on earth are you talking about?' She was entirely confused by the woman's deliberate delivery and muffled tone, as if she had her hand over the mouthpiece.

'You'd be an absolute rubbish spy.' Her friend stated.

'Well, I wasn't planning on a career change so that's not a bad thing.'

'I was talking in code.'

'If you say so!'

'They've left. The three of them should be in town in about ten minutes.'

'Thanks honey. And thank you for yesterday. You made us all so welcome, Jack too.' She meant it.

'That's what friends are for. Anyway, I only really called to say let me know how it goes today. Especially between you and the very lovely Professor Clever Clogs.'

'I don't think there'll be anything to tell.' She smiled at his impromptu nickname.

'Oh, I'm not so sure, there were a few sparks flying yesterday! Even Jack noticed.'

'He did?' The thought thrilled her.

'Yes, and considering my husband is the kind of man that unless I'm *dressed* like a fish, *talking* about fishing, or are actually *preparing* fish to eat, doesn't really give me his full attention, it's really quite incisive of him.'

'He called me gorgeous.' Her blush bloomed over her chest and neck, she felt stupid saying it, what were they, teens?

'Wowserooney! Gorgeous, eh? That's high level. Should we be saving up for new hats, preparing for another trip up the aisle?'

'Oh, Good Lord above no! That didn't even happen the first time around...'

'But I notice you aren't saying no to a second time around? If things went in that direction? Or am I prying too much?'

'You are definitely prying too much!' She smiled, secretly a little thrilled by the very unlikely prospect, 'and as much as I'm fond of Bill, and I am, I think that ship has sailed. I'm too old for all that.'

'That's what I used to think.' Verity confirmed.

'Besides, it's all about Knox and Ashley right now.'

'You're right of course, let me know how today goes, Gorgeous!'

'I will!'

Verity's words had enthused and energised her. *Sparks!* That's what she'd said! With her purse over her shoulder, grinning like a Cheshire cat and wearing another crisp blouse to complement her jeans, she made her way into town with a spring in her step.

It was as she drew closer, that she slowed her pace, having spied the trio already in situ, standing by the grand old Linden tree. It was a moment when she wondered about that different life, one where she'd stayed and watched her son vault from boy to man, where to walk into town to meet her family might be the norm. Her stomach rolled with loss at all she had missed, having made the decision to follow her head and not her heart.

'Will you look at this place!' Ashley twirled on the grass by the tree with her arms spread wide, 'It's like something from a book! It's so cute!'

'It is.' She felt the flicker of nerves when looking at her son, their fraught exchange fresh in her thoughts from yesterday. 'How did y'all sleep?'

'Like logs!' Ashley sighed, 'although some of us like logs who snore very, very loudly!' She jerked her head in Knox' direction.

'You can talk! Thought a freight train was coming right on through!' He could clearly give as good as he got.

'You are so not funny.' Ashley pulled a face, 'anyway, enough of this, let's get this day started and I need to start it by going to the bookstore,' Ashley pointed at Town Books – 'you coming hon?' She prodded Knox in the side.

'Is that okay, if we wander off, Mom?' He asked softly, and she heard apology in his tone.

'Of course. You guys take your time.' She felt nothing but love for him.

54

'Don't you worry about us.' Bill settled back into one of the benches that lined the town square. 'We'll sit here and soak up the sunshine!'

Vera took the seat next to him and it was a space that she filled with ease, this proximity familiar and warming. Again, it made her wonder what life would have been like if this was just a regular day in Linden Falls, with her and Bill going about that business, like Verity and Jack or Pam and Steve, couples who just seemed to work. The beat of silence was far from awkward and something she had quite forgotten, how at ease they were in each other's company and how the quiet moments were as good as the chatter-filled ones. It was Bill who finally broke the impasse, and his words were deep and thought provoking, not the idle small talk she had been expecting with weather and traffic at the fore.

'It's hard parenting a grown-up, isn't it? I mean I know they're responsible adults, but there are times when he and Ashley both seem so young to me.' Bill spoke softly as he watched the two wander towards the book store hand in hand.

'Maybe you're just getting old.' She sighed.

'No maybe about it. My back after any night on a strange mattress likes to remind me of just that.' He stretched and winced.

'And do you find yourself often sleeping on strange mattresses?'

She asked with a hint of humour, but it was also enquiring, did he still date? She was curious, remembering what Knox had said about how he wished his dad would get out there and what was the name of the woman he was trying to arrange a date with, Melissa? Was that it? Well, in that moment she was glad Melissa hadn't been able to organise her diary to go out for dinner, and was far, far away...

Bill turned to face her, 'Not as many as I'd like! Although recently...'

'Recently what?' She asked coyly.

'Let's just say it turns out there's life in the old dog yet!'

They both laughed. Taking a moment to study the other's face at close range. Her heart soared, as excitement fizzed in her veins, was he talking about her?

'It seems like life is being kind to you V.'

'It is. I'm happy here.'

'That's good to hear, good to hear.' He paused, as if weighing up his words, 'It was never easy for me, you know,'

'What wasn't?' She prompted.

'It was never easy for me, knowing I didn't make you happy. Knowing I couldn't give you what you needed.'

'But you did.' She met his gaze. 'You did make me happy, Bill. The happiest!' She felt her heart rate increase.

'That's easy to say, but I think your actions speak differently and history will think of it differently. I've never known anyone living in bliss just up and go!' He made a darting motion with his hand.

'Why is it still so hard for me to talk about, even after twenty odd years, why would I still rather talk about anything than those days?' Her honesty tripped from her tongue.

'Guilt? Regret? Little bit of both?' He suggested.

'Guilt definitely. Regret possibly.' She ran her finger under her nose, as emotion threatened. 'It wasn't easy for me Bill and not only because of the obvious reasons, giving up you, taking Knox away. It was also frustrating, being the only one who could look ahead and see how it ended, how I would hold you back, how you'd grow tired of me, of us...'

'V, I had absolutely no idea!' He turned to face her with a shake of disbelief to his head. 'And how fortunate are you? It's a wonderful, wonderful thing! I honestly had no idea! Wow!' He spoke loudly, and she shrunk back a little, alarmed by his response and his volume, concerned that any one of her customers or neighbours could be within ear shot. It was only his next words that revealed he was being sarcastic. 'So come on, where is this magic crystal ball that shows you the future and my God, how I could have done with an advantage like that over the years! Let's see now,' he drummed his mouth with his fingers, as if in thought. 'Lottery numbers, future health scares that could have been avoided. Oh, and I could have told Des Monroe, one of my neighbours, to look twice before stepping off the sidewalk, could have *warned* him that the bus driver would at the exact same moment be reaching for his meatball sub and that poor Des would end up six feet under instead of coming with me to watch the baseball. Could I borrow it do you think? Not only do I want to see how my shares are going to do, which will in turn determine what vacation I next book, but I'm also halfway through a box set and time's a little tight. If I can borrow your crystal ball, look ahead, reveal the twist and be done with it, save me a heck of a lot of watching time!'

'You're not funny.' She folded her arms over her chest.

'Well, we don't need a crystal ball to confirm that.' He chuckled wryly, his voice and manner, calmer now, 'but it's true V, you talk with such certainty, but the fact is, you *didn't* know. You couldn't know! Instead, you made a judgment call based on no more than your own prejudice, your own issues and you took Knox, and you went. You left me and I was... broken. Completely broken...'

'Me too.' She whispered.

'I'd listened for the longest time to stories of your life, how you'd cut and run so many times before. You always spoke so openly about it that I figured it must be cathartic, never in a million years thinking it was possible where we were concerned. I thought that we, as a couple, were healing each other of past wrongs and anxieties. I thought we were stronger than that. I thought we were different.' He held her eye line, 'but we weren't different. We weren't strong and we weren't enough. Because you did what you've always done, jumped before you

57

were pushed. You ran. Just like you'd run from your folks, run from the place you grew up, your family, your school friends, your town… You ran from me, from *me!*' He placed his hand on his chest, 'and then ran from wherever you were before here,'

'Tulsa.' She filled in the gap.

'Oh yes that's right, Tulsa. And here seems nice, but,' he looked around, taking in the picket fences and neat cut lawns.

'But what?'

'How long? How long until you bolt, V?'

To hear her life laid out in such simple terms without any of the reasons that drove her actions was far from easy. To hear of his distress and how he had crumpled after she went, even harder.

'You always used to say, "*If you don't like the world you are in, build a better one…*" and I have. I want to stay here. I have my business, good friends, I'm happy,'

'I did used to say that. And yet it sounds like there's a 'but' coming?'

She shook her head. 'You think you have me all figured out.'

'Oh no,' he shook his head, 'I've never had you all figured out. If I had, I'd have known how to make you stay.'

His words slid down her throat like broken glass. She bit her lip and stared up at the beautiful Linden tree whose leaves ruffled in the breeze, providing a soft, shifting music that was soothing, a reminder that this tree was alive!

'I have found peace V, peace and happiness. And I think,' his voice was low now, sincere, 'that what you're running from is inside you and so no matter where you go or how great your new neighbourhood, you are only going to take it with you. You can't outrun it no matter how many times you start over. Happiness and acceptance, they aren't a destination. They are a state of mind, a self-belief.'

His words rang high and true and were all the more painful because of it. Bill wasn't done.

'And in my humble opinion, as someone who always had and always *will* hold you in the greatest affection, I think you would benefit from being kinder to yourself, from letting go of the negative thoughts. You should pour water on the embers I watched you stoke until flames raged and destroyed whatever happiness and peace you had in the present. You deserve for it to stop. You deserve love, peace, and happiness! That's the goal for all of us, right?'

Love, peace, and happiness... She closed her eyes and pictured these words as the Linden rustled loudly as if in response.

'I'd like that, Bill.' She pictured the blood of rabbits and razorbacks, dripping onto the porch, her brothers rolling around in the yard with split lips and black eyes, her dad's drunken shouting as he made his way home, loud enough to wake the whole neighbourhood. And her momma sat in that reclining chair, raising the volume on the TV while hollering, '*Sweet Mother of Betsy will you two quit!*' 'Yes, I'd like that very much.'

He sat forward and with his hands joined on his knees and his head a little bowed, he looked to be in prayer, 'you and me V. We have things to talk about. Things I want to talk about, things I need to talk about.'

Her heart leapt at just the possibility that there might still be something to explore between her and the only man she had ever loved. Not only did she feel joy at the prospect of a new and exciting love, but also, she wanted more than anything to put things right, to take what she had broken and fix it, fix them!

'I think, I think that's a very good idea.'

She stared at him, waiting to hear his idea, his suggestion, knowing she would let him finish what it was he needed to say, but knowing that whatever he was about to suggest - her answer was going to be,

'Yes! Yes! Let's try again, let's spend some time, let's see what lies ahead for an old couple like you and me! One more time around the block Billy! Let's do it!'

'Hey!' Ashley called and drew them from their conversation. It took all of Vera's strength to abandon her chat with Bill and turn her attention to Ashley, knowing she wouldn't rest until the conversation could be continued.

'Look what I made?'

In the girl's hand she had a tray loaded with glorious baked goods. What looked to be big fat croissant, fudgy brownies, and a couple of raspberry tarts, the fruit dotted neatly into the pale sunshine coloured custard. Knox walked by her side with takeaway cups. She and Bill laughed; their future daughter-in-law was funny.

'So, I see you found the Cobblestone bakery?' She smiled, partly because the prospect of fresh baked goods was enticing, but mainly because after just half an hour in Bill's company, his thought-provoking words very much in line with her own thoughts and regrets; smiling felt like the easiest thing in the world!

'I love this place! I love it so much!' Ashley beamed, sitting down on the grass in front of the bench and folding her legs before handing around the cakes, while Knox gave them each a hot cup of coffee.

'Everyone here knows you, Mom.' He smiled with something that looked a lot like pride. 'One mention and they all had such nice things to say. It's really cool.'

'It's a small place, and I am the only salon in town, so it'd be hard to be anonymous.'

'I'd love to see it!' Ashley took a huge bite of brownie and spoke with her mouthful, 'Jeez this is so good!'

'It's only small,' Vera felt the familiar flicker of nerves at the prospect of taking these three to see her little business.

They were smart, they were professors! And she spent her days mixing tint... She hated how the cloak of inadequacy wrapped itself around her tightly. Bill was right, she needed to be kinder to herself, needed to let go of negative thoughts. If only doing it was as easy as saying it.

'I'd still like to visit.' Ashley pushed.

'Sure, we can nip in if you like.' She sipped her coffee and broke the end of a croissant, the flaky, buttery pastry almost melted on her tongue, it was delicious.

'I'll come too.' Knox added his enthusiasm.

'And me!' Bill added.

'Well, all right then.' With the three all sharing such enthusiasm, she felt she had no choice other than to march forward and prepare for her two worlds to collide. It took all of her strength to keep her voice steady and halt the tremble of her fingers at the prospect.

MIRA DID a double take as the bell above the front door chimed. Vera, quick to reassure the girl that she was not checking up on her and with nerves fuelling her speech, babbled a little,

'Hey darlin'. Well, here it is! As I said, it's small!' She hated how she did the place a disservice, her words giving no clue to just how much she loved it and how proud she was of it. 'And this is Mira who does a fine job, and that's Ms Mary May under the dryer,' the lady raised her hand in a small wave, distracted briefly from her magazine as she was.

'Hi!' Mira smiled at the gang who now filled the salon.

'Hi, I'm Ashley, Knox's fiancée, it still feels weird to say that *fiancée*!'

Mira looked a little giddy. She had confided in Vera a while ago that becoming a fiancée was one of her goals in life, with the express intention of it leading to the title of "wife". It had made Vera wonder why it had never been one of her goals?

'And I'm Knox, Vera's son.' He stepped forward and Vera felt her heart flutter, he was actually here in her little salon, her boy...

'This is so great!' Vera was learning that Ashley carried extraordinary enthusiasm for most new things, it was as endearing as it was infectious.

'It's a pleasure to meet you all, and so good to...' Mira faltered, 'good to see you out and about!' The girl blushed, as nerves coated her tongue.

Vera smiled. She had told Mira that her son was coming to visit but hadn't thought to quash the gossip that he had been incarcerated, or worse.

'Thanks.' Polite as ever, she caught the look of bemusement he and Ashley exchanged.

'And you work here with my mom?' Knox made small talk.

'Uh-huh, I love my job. Love working with your mom.' The girl's words made Vera's heart swell with affection. 'Are you all heading over to Vera's place now?' Mira asked in all innocence, and why would she suppose anything different?

'Well, that sounds perfect!' Sweet Ashley smiled at her. 'Let's do that! Tell me you have photo albums of when this one was a baby.' She snaked her arm around Knox' waist and squeezed him tightly.

'Sure! Let's do that.' Vera felt the ping of uncertainty in her stomach and wished she'd given the air one more spray with her favoured Febreze.

The sound of Knox' laughter caught them all off guard.

'What's so funny?' Ashley looked as perplexed as Vera felt.

'I've just realised, Vera and Mira – you sound like a circus double act or those twins who dress alike and live together – professional twins!'

To her relief Mira joined in. 'I'd quite like a life in the circus. I've seen the Greatest Showman and I loved it!'

'Oh, come on honey, life here can be a hoot! Why would you want to go anywhere else?' Vera did what she did best, chatted, smiled, and found her happy. 'Besides, I don't think all circuses have a Hugh Jackman in them, sorry to disappoint.'

'Then I'm afraid you're stuck with me, Vera.' The girl radiated joy as if at the thought of it and it filled Vera with warmth. 'I shall grow old here and you can nap out back while I cut Mrs Darby's hair and mix up the tints!'

'Growing old together, now wouldn't that be something.' Bill had been a little quiet, as if taking in the event but not feeling quite part of it and not for the first time, Vera wondered what it might have been that he was going to say when Ashley appeared, weighed down with cakes... He now spoke with an edge of jest, but his words were almost melancholic.

It was however yet another crumb he threw, suggesting they were not done. He spoke so publicly that her first reaction was to look towards Knox to see if he bristled at his father's words. Quite the contrary, he didn't seem to feel their impact and instead stared at Ashley, as if picturing growing old with the girl *he* loved.

Mira looked a little sheepish, she, unlike Knox seemed fully aware. Vera felt the uncomfortable slide of exposure over her skin as her personal life and business life collided.

But to speak of growing old together... How did it make her feel? The answer came quickly: unbelievably happy! And if it could work out for Verity and Jack and even Neva and Henry – why not her and Bill?

Leaving Mira to run the salon, the four of them trooped along the lane, her nerves swelled until they filled her up more than the giant croissant, she had polished off earlier. Her plan had been to show them around town and then suggest lunch at the Crooked Porch, or a picnic by the lake, or sandwiches on the deck of the cabin at "White Cedar Farm". This impromptu visit had rather thrown her.

'Here we are, just up ahead.'

She walked along the lane until they came to the pretty park where her neat trailer nestled among trees, next to Mrs Kenny's and with six more up along the track. 'These buildings used to be ski lodges for wintering visitors, but they were sold back in the eighties, made into permanent homes, and here we are.'

'Cute!' Ashley closed her eyes, 'it's *so* cute and so close to town. It's great.'

Ashley, it seemed, thought that most things were cute. Vera caught Bill's eye and saw the smallest suggestion of a smile. She had no doubt that if they were more familiar with each other, if the years hadn't been erased, it would have been a full-blown eye roll. She liked to think so.

The four climbed up onto the deck, as Vera fished in her bag for her door key. Out of the corner of her eye, she saw the swish of Mrs Kenny's lace curtain and silently thanked the old lady for watching over the front door for any odd activity, which was what good neighbours did.

'Don't look now,' Ashley whispered, 'but I think we are being watched!' She tilted her head towards Mrs Kenny's trailer.

'Oh, don't mind her none, she's a sweet lady who keeps an eye on the place. She has a hot tub on her rear deck.' She wasn't sure why she added the detail.

'You don't say?' Ashley's question carried a whiff of sarcasm, and it bothered Vera. Again, she and Bill shared a knowing look.

'This is it!' Not for the first time that day, she stood back and opened up the small space she so loved to people she knew she didn't have to impress, and yet still the feeling of being so very ordinary threatened to drag her down.

Knox walked in and smiled, as he looked around, Ashley walked ahead.

'Mom, if you dropped me in here in a blindfold and told me nothing, I'd know this was your place.'

'Aside from the photos of you everywhere you mean?' She pointed to the collection in glass frames of him at various stages, from toddler to teen, all beaming the same big smile right at the camera.

'If I wasn't in a blindfold, sure, but it's more than that. It's so neat, clean, and tidy and smells like flowers. It's what I always think about when I picture being younger. Even those little rooms we had in Tallahassee,' Vera felt her brow fold at the memory of that year, working as a hairdresser by day in one of the big hotels and waitressing at night, while girls she worked with watched over Knox when she worked a shift outside of school hours or it was night time. She didn't know how much of it he might remember, how old had he been, seven, eight? He wasn't done. 'Yeah, even in those little rooms where we shared a bathroom down the hall with other families, you used to bring fresh flowers in and put them in a jar in the middle of the wobbly kitchen table and they were the first thing you'd see when you walked in and the last thing you'd see before you fell asleep. You made the place beautiful.'

'As beautiful as I could.' The lump in her throat made speech a little tricky.

'Yes, Mom, as beautiful as you could.'

Vera wondered if her son would ever know the power of his memory, acknowledging not only her desire to make his home pretty, but also that he didn't mention the damp in the bathroom, the filthy walls, the broken door handles, fights that could be heard through the paper-thin walls in the early hours, the boarded-up windows or communal hallways that stank of human misery. No, he remembered the flowers she would pick from verges or take from the hotel dumpster where she knew she could eeek them out for another couple of days.

It occurred to her then that if he thought this was their world, if this was how he remembered things, a world of flowers and prettiness, of joy and security, no wonder he might have found it hard to understand her choice to send him to go live with his dad. No wonder he'd flared and suggested she had 'given him away.' His kind words right now, however, meant the whole world and it was just as she was figuring out how best to reply that Ashley's scream caused them all to run along the little hallway.

Ashley had found the bedroom and stood with Miss Emilia-Jane in her hand. Vera fought the compulsion to remove the doll from her, wary of her not being handled right. She was delicate and precious, to her at least.

'Now Vera, please tell me these creatures are not from a horror movie! Sweet Lord they are so scary! Look at their faces! I wouldn't sleep if these haunted things were under my roof!'

She made out to shove the Miss Emilia-Jane towards Knox and the doll's fancy wide brimmed hat flopped forward. Vera felt rooted to the spot, overcome with emotion and conflicted. She didn't want her dolls touched, and certainly didn't want them mocked. Bill stepped forward and took Miss Emilia-Jane from his future daughter-in-law. He restored the doll's hat and put her next to her sisters.

'I think we shouldn't be rooting around in a lady's bedroom.'

'I think you're right.' Knox backed his dad, and all felt weighted by the blanket of awkwardness that descended.

'God, sorry!' Ashley, knitted her hands and looked more than a little awkward, 'I was only trying to put everyone at their ease, make myself at home.'

'And you are most welcome to make yourself at home.' Vera held the girl's eyeline, but the unspoken words rang around her head like a siren, *but don't touch my dolls without asking and then only with the utmost respect.* 'Now who wants a cool drink?'

After enjoying lemonade on the deck, where Bill admired her thriving plants and she bloomed in being able to give him the detail and particular care routine of each variety, showing off not only the results but also her horticultural knowledge, the four made their way back into town.

Walking in couples with Knox and Ashley in front, she watched how her son chatted calmly to his fiancée with his arm about her shoulders, whether advising, placating, or reassuring, it was hard to hear, but either way, she looked up at him with an expression of humility. Knox it seemed might have felt as strongly as his dad about Ashley's treatment of Miss Emilia-Jane and she was glad, feeling that their reaction justified her own level of upset at the over-familiar action. This was not how she wanted their day in Linden Falls to end, not how she wanted to remember this rare and precious visit,

'We should get lunch and sit under the Linden tree – how about that? I don't do it often enough, but to sit and let life in the town square pass all around is a wonderful thing to do. What do you think?'

'I think that sounds like a plan.' Knox called over his shoulder, reaching for Ashley's hand as he did so.

Having stuffed their faces with fresh baguettes fully loaded with salad, a decent spicy mayonnaise and hand carved slices of thick country ham, the four lay back on the grass with full stomachs. The sunlight dappled through the wide branches and bathed them in filtered light.

'I love it here.' Ashley spoke softly and Vera got the impression the young girl was trying to smooth the path, restore trust and well meaning. Her heart went out to her. She was only young and while she might be academic and know all there was about oceans and whatnot, she clearly had a lot of life experience to pick up. She decided to pick up the thread and weave her own words of healing, forgiveness, and reconciliation, knowing the last thing she wanted her future daughter-in-law to feel was awkward.

'There's something about it, isn't there Ashley?' she sat up, looking at the girl directly, 'I remember I only intended to pass through,'

Bill made a humph noise which she chose to ignore.

'Thought I'd stay for a couple of days and head up state, all my belongings in my old truck.' Her face broke into a smile to think of that day. 'I came here, sat just over there on a bench,' she pointed, 'and the breeze was warm and the ribbons with all the messages fluttered on the branches, and it felt...' It was a struggle to find the right word, 'magical.' Yes, that was the word. *Magical.* 'One of the first people I met was Neva who owns the Inn. She asked me where I was from and I kept it vague, told her here and there and she laughed, then she handed me a long bobby pin, the kind we used to cram into our hair as teenagers to achieve a look, the kind our mothers used to have in a jar on their vanity unit.' Her own mother's stash had sat in a grubby drawer, not that she was about to share that. 'And I'll never forget she said, is this yours? And I took it into my hand, and it made me smile as she had no way of knowing I was a hairdresser, and yet there it was, an old-fashioned bobby pin.'

'Weird.' Knox murmured.

'A bit weird yes, but also kind of welcoming and it made me think. Made me think about my life, what I love doing, what I needed at that time in my life.'

'Did you make a wish on the tree?' Ashley asked sweetly.

'I did.'

Vera remembered that wish like it was yesterday, *'please let me find peace. Give me roots to keep me steady and a warm wind to lift my spirits...'*

'Did it come true?' Bill almost whispered.

As a breeze rustled the abundant leaves and flowed over her warm skin, she smiled.

'Uh huh.'

'I'm going to make a wish!' Ashley jumped up, 'Knox, go grab me one of the labels and the pen from the little box,' both of which they had discovered earlier. 'I want to do it now! Right now!'

She watched as Knox loped up, wiped grass from the seat of his pants and fetched a label on a ribbon and the marker pen.

Ashley worked quickly, writing furiously, and tying her wish, along with others to flutter at will.

'I want to shout my wish from the rooftops!' The girl spoke excitedly.

'Don't do that it might never come true.' Vera counselled.

Bill backed her up, 'Wishes should definitely not be told.'

'I hear ya!' Ashley put her hands on her hips, 'but sometimes if you don't tell they don't come true either and my wish is this,' without further ado, she spoke clearly and confidently, calling her wish into the ether, 'I want to get married right here in Linden Falls. I don't want to wait for a big wedding with planning and perfection. *Here* is perfect. Right here in Linden Falls. This is where we should do it Knox, I can feel it and I don't want to wait. I want to get married here!'

'What do you think Mom?' Knox spoke as if seeking permission and she knew it was an honor in every sense.

'I...' The words stuck in her throat, 'I... I don't know what to say!'

This was the truth as any delight was edged out with sheer terror at the thought of hosting the wedding and having to greet Ashley's old-fashioned parents, how would that work?

'Well, I think It's a fine idea,' Bill it seemed was keen to give *his* permission and apparently this sealed the deal. 'An excuse to come back, to come back here to this fantastic place.'

Bill held her eye line, as Knox scooped his bride to be off the ground into a warm hug before kissing her face, 'That's what you want? That's your wish?'

'It really is.' Ashley nodded.

Knox put her back on solid ground. 'Well, I think that's one wish we can all help make come true, with or without the aid of the tree!' He turned to Vera who felt stunned, excited, nervous and stunned. 'Mom, do Verity and Jack ever hold events up at White Cedar Farm, I'm thinking nothing too fancy, but a dinner, bit of a dance, haybales to sit on and a willing pastor?'

'I could ask!' She decided to do just that.

'Oh Knox!' Ashley bit her knuckles, 'is this really happening?'

'Looks like it.'

Her son looked at her and there was the faintest glimmer of something in his expression that caused the breath to catch in her throat, what was it? She would have found it hard to voice, and it was gone in an instant. It was only later when she properly considered the moment that she realised he had looked a bit like her, right before she decided to bolt.

CHAPTER 6

*V*erity stepped forward and placed her arm around Vera's shoulders, she patted the back of her friend's hand, glad of the support as they stood side by side on the porch of White Cedar Farm and waved the visitors off. It had been one heck of a few days. Bill drove the hire car, as Ashley, with her small pillow in her hand, prepared to sleep on the back seat, and Knox, had reluctantly agreed to keep his "old man" company up front.

It might have only been a matter of weeks until they returned, but still she felt the familiar lurch in her heart at parting. This coupled with a low-lying resentment as the three headed off together, and she was once again left on the sidelines, watching, as they set off for a life in which she had no part. She reminded herself that this was her decision, it was her that had run all those years ago, knowing that her actions would come with consequences, some harder than others. And this was one of them. The fact that she was living the life she had chosen and carved for herself, however, cut very little ice when she longed to be in that car.

Saying goodbye had been bittersweet, sharp hugs for Knox and Ashley with excited burbles about the following few weeks, wedding plans to be discussed, emails to look out for, hurried reminders about flowers and cake, all swept up in the heady joy of frantic planning and with Verity and Jack grinning, seemingly happy to have been given the role of hosts. Vera knew she would never be able to repay their kindness, their friendship.

Saying good bye to Bill had been a little different. It wasn't in the least bit hurried or overcrowded with words and promises of hastily thought up wedding tasks. It was instead calm, quiet, and meaningful. He had stepped off the porch and stood on the ground, looking directly at her, their eyes almost level. Without any awkwardness, he had taken both of her hands into his and there they stood, staring at each other in the way they had done so often in their youth at bus stops, on the steps of their faculty supplied apartment or on beaches. Saying goodbye back then had always been accompanied by long, hard, desperate kisses that smacked of reunion and were full of promise of all that lay ahead for the young couple. As if parting, even for the shortest while, was almost unbearable.

As Knox had loaded up the trunk and Ashley had swept the cabin to make sure they'd left nothing behind, Bill had spoken softly.

'So, V,' he'd begun, and she waited to hear the words that she felt had been on the tip of his tongue when they'd been interrupted by Ashley's shout on their day out.

'...you and me V. We have things to talk about. Things I want to talk about. Things I need to talk about.'

Even the memory of what he'd said and the way he'd said it, enough to make her gut flip with something very close to excitement.

'So, Bill.' She countered.

'I guess I'll see you in a couple of weeks.' He smiled and bit his bottom lip in the way she knew he did when he had something of merit to say, some news to share, words of wisdom to impart, and her heart jumped.

'I guess you will.' She flicked her hair from her face, as she had when she was a teen and there was longer hair to flick.

'We should catch up then, properly. Finish that conversation.'

Leaning forward he kissed her sweetly on the cheek and with his words and the image they conjured filling her up so much, it made speech almost impossible. Almost.

'I shall look forward to it.' He managed.

He had winked, as her hands slipped from his and after thanking Jack and Verity for the final time, he'd strode to the car and climbed in.

And here she was, waving as the wheels kicked up a cloud of dust as the car rattled around the bend and out of view.

'Sparks!' Verity spoke wistfully, 'what do you think Jack?'

'Yup. Sparks. No doubt.'

Vera smiled over her shoulder at them.

'Fancy a cup of tea?' Verity joined her, staring at the gap where the car had only recently departed.

'I think I'll get on home Verity but thank you and you Jack for everything. What would I do without you both?'

'Well, I jolly well hope you never have to find out!' Her friend's sweet reminder that they weren't going anywhere. 'Anyway, I shall see you in the week, we have a wedding to plan!' She clapped her hands, 'so exciting! I'm going to give Jack a list of everything that needs painting, fences, gates that sort of thing.'

Jack, an artist by trade shook his head, 'I might have guessed that all the manual work would fall into my lap.'

'I'll make it up to you.' She made big eyes in his direction.

'Apple pie with cinnamon syrup?' His demeanour lifted at the question alone.

'You bet, and cream.' His wife nodded.

'It's true what they say Vera, the way to a man's heart is through his stomach!'

'So that's where I've been going wrong.' She quipped.

'I'm off into town,' Jack smiled, 'meeting Wyatt to go through the lease.'

'Who's Wyatt?' It was a name new to her.

'Jack's picture framer friend from Colorado is relocating, he's going to have a gallery out front, give Jack's work somewhere to be shown and sold locally, and he'll frame pictures out the back.'

'Well, that's exciting! And just what Linden Falls needs, a gallery – how wonderful.'

'Yes, and nice for Jack to have his buddy around. Wyatt has been through the ringer a bit.'

'That's a shame.' She didn't pry but knew her sympathies were with anyone who had had a rough time. Verity volunteered the information anyway.

'His wife died a couple of years ago and he kind of went to ground, so this is a fresh start for him, new place, new business...'

'That sounds familiar.' Vera thought back to her own arrival over a decade ago and how with Bill's arrival she might be willing to pack up again and head off to wherever he was. It was a thought that was as thrilling as it was terrifying.

'He's a nice guy. Deserves the break.'

'Well, if Linden Falls is good at one thing, it's making new arrivals feel welcome! And I can testify to that.'

'Me too!' Verity chuckled.

Vera made her way to her old truck, keys in hand. Verity walked with her and when she spoke her voice was calm, quiet.

'What's going on with you and Bill? Because from what I saw today, it was like you guys just picked up where you left off, all very flirty. And a little bit hand holdy.'

Vera liked her quirky way of phrasing things.

'He said we have things to talk about and I think he might be right.'

'And don't forget the gorgeous bit, he said you were gorgeous too!' Her friend enthused, and the two giggled like teens sharing gossip on prom night and fanning the flames of anticipation. It felt good to know that someone else had picked up the attraction that she feared she might have imagined, such was her lack of confidence.

Vera paused, taking a slow breath, 'Yes he did say that. It feels easy with him, Verity, it always did.'

'So, what went wrong? Because to you see you two together, you'd never think that anything could have been serious enough to pull you apart.'

'It was down to me, I guess. I ran out on him, and I took Knox, pretty much as I told you before they arrived, but,' she ran her fingers over the back of her other hand as if still able to feel the touch of the man she had once so loved, 'seeing him, it reminds me of all that was good. Plus, I'm a different person now, and I'm beginning to think that I might believe in second chances...' *Might believe in myself...*

'Wowsers!'

'Yes, wowsers. But hey, there's a lot of water to go under a lot of bridges before then and in the meantime, we have a weddin' to plan!'

'We sure do.'

'Do you think Knox is happy?' Vera turned to look at her friend, as if this required nothing less than her full attention.

'I'd say so. He and Ashley are obviously keen as mustard and he seemed to have led the march when it came to the wedding, very involved. Why do you ask, do you think differently?'

'I don't know,' Vera proceeded with caution, wary of sounding like an over-protective or judgemental mom. 'There was just something in his eyes that made me wonder.

Only briefly, but a hesitancy, as if the importance of the decision he's making is only just dawning on him.'

'Or maybe you're projecting a little, worried because of how you would feel in that situation?' Verity asked tentatively.

'Yes, possibly. I hope so, I mean it's not great to admit, but better that than him rushing headlong only to repent at leisure, as they say.'

'They do indeed. But I really don't think you have anything to worry about.' Verity shifted foot to foot, as if a little nervous, 'can... can I ask you something?'

'Of course.' She listened, as if sensing her friend's seriousness.

'It's something I've wanted to ask you for a while,'

'Well now's as good a time as any!' Vera was starting to feel the lap of nerves, wanting Verity to spit it out. Whatever 'it' was.

'You always seem so happy, so positive,'

'I try.' This was the truth.

'A couple of years ago, Jack and I were out walking in the town square one evening. It had been snowing heavily and we went out to mooch around and look at the Christmas decorations, it was that holiday when my daughter came home to surprise me, do you remember? When Jack arranged the whole thing and got me out of the house on some fool's errand, and when I got back, there she was with her dad and Freya, who's now her stepmom. And who was pregnant at the time with little Monty.'

'I remember!' She did indeed.

'Well, I never said anything at the time and haven't since, but,' Verity paused, 'Jack and I were walking along, arm in arm, and we saw you by the wishing tree.'

Verity tensed, knowing what her friend was going to say, unaware that she'd been seen.

'It was cold, quite dark and yet you were knelt in the

snow. Huddled forward, I could tell you were weeping, distressed. It was jarring to see you - the usually vivacious woman who is always so sunny, bent and sobbing. I honestly didn't know what to do.'

Vera nodded, embarrassed that her friend had seen her this way at such a low moment.

'It was so unlike you. I remember asking Jack, what we should do? We didn't want to interfere, didn't want to pry, and yet wanted to check on you. And I never said as much to Jack, but I was also wary of disturbing you. You looked so lost to your sorrow, so wrapped up in the moment, and having had my own fair share of heartache, I know that sometimes those moments can actually be quite cathartic. I was torn.'

'It was sweet of you to worry, Verity.'

'We were just about to walk over when we spied Neva at the window of the inn. She shook her head at us, as if letting us know that she was right there, that she'd got the situation in hand. So, we kept on walking, but I never forgot the sight of you in the snow like that. What was it Vera that affected you so badly, if you don't mind me asking?'

She felt the tremble of her bottom lip, just the memory of that time enough to fill her with emotion. 'It's simple really. I don't like the holidays.' There she had said it. 'I mean sure the cookies are great, carolers fun, I don't even mind the odd slice of turkey and I'm a sucker for a good Hallmark movie with a glass of eggnog, curled up on the couch, but Christmas time has always been hard for me.' It felt hard even after all this time to think about those days, 'when I was a kid I lived on a knife edge around Christmas. Santa always missed us off his list and that sucked. But it was more than that.' She swallowed, 'and not that my family needed an excuse to cut loose but, in the holidays, there was more beer flowing and maybe a little more cash and that meant a little more chaos, a little more violence.'

'Oh Vera!' Verity let her head fall to one side and her expression was one of sympathy.

'But that's not why I was crying, why I always cry then.' She took a breath, 'Knox was born on December 24th. And since the day I took him to go live with Bill, I've found the day almost intolerable. I keep it together, do what I can throughout the year to distract me from the fact that he's so far away,'

'That happy face.' Verity cut in.

'Yep, that happy face. But on his birthday, you're right, sorrow wraps around me so tightly it almost suffocates me. So yes, he was born on Christmas Eve, and I always take my sorry self up to the Linden tree and I throw myself on the ground at its mercy. I ask it to keep my boy safe and I think about all the things I thought when I first held him, first looked into this little face. I wished for him a good life, a happy life, a healthy life and so I guess those wishes came true and I'm thankful. He is all of those things and more. But the feeling in my stomach like I've been hollowed out by our separation.' She swallowed, 'yes, it's a hard holiday for me.'

'I think...' Verity took her time, 'I think everyone at times doubts themselves, thinks they might not be up to the mark.'

Vera knew where this was heading, 'but what if I don't *think* I'm not up to the mark, what if I *know* it?'

'Then learn to un-know it. Learn to doubt that interior monologue that reinforces all the rubbish ideas you hold on to, because they're not true.' She stared at her friend, 'when my husband Sonny had that very public affair, I thought I'd never lift my head in public again. I knew some people were laughing at me, others pitying me and some even taking joy in my misfortune and I let those thoughts race around my head, keeping me awake at night. Then, one day, I realised, it was up to me to change the way I thought, up to me to ignore all of them, not pay heed to any other opinion. As my daughter is fond of saying "you do you." And she's right.

Everyone else can go to hell with whatever they think or whatever it is they think they know. The only opinion that counts is your own and if you don't mind me saying,'

'Go ahead, you haven't exactly held back up to this point!' Vera reminded her.

'True, and so if you don't mind me saying, you might *feel* like you shouldn't have run all those years ago, might even regret your choices, might feel like you have been missing out because of how things are now. I saw your face when you waved them off, but the point is; it's not too late to change how you feel, Vera. It's not too late to go after the life you missed out on. Not too late to have a little bit more faith in yourself. If you don't like the world you live in,'

'Make it a better one.'

'Exactly. And you deserve it all. You're wonderful and smart and add such positivity to the lives of all of us, you make everyone feel good! And I think… I think it's time you let yourself feel good too.'

Vera nodded, wondering if her friend was right, could she change how she felt about herself, wash off the stink of the Delaney name and let herself fall again for the man who had promised her the whole wide world?

'Thank you, Verity.'

The two women fell into a sincere hug. It was certainly a lot to think about.

VERA WOUND DOWN THE WINDOW, letting the warm evening breeze lift her hair and her spirits. With her friend's words racing in her thoughts, she slowly wound along the lanes and dropped down into Linden Falls, heading home.

The violet light from Mrs Kenny's TV screen filtered through her window and lit the porch with its glow. And even though she had left her home and everything in it as neat as a pin, the galley kitchen sparkling, the fringed rug in front of the couch straightened, and not a speck of dust on the shelves around her wide TV, everything just right – still she felt the pull of desolation. The sight of her surroundings tonight didn't bring joy like it usually did. Instead, compared to the easy chatter of Knox and Ashley in the background and the presence of Bill, she felt the ache of loneliness, as the quiet pulsed around her.

'I want a better world.' She spoke softly to her reflection in the mirror, 'I *want* more. I want my family and I think I want Bill.'

Just the admission was enough to make her smile. Yes, she wanted Bill and she wanted to be closer to Knox. No matter how unpalatable, he spoke the truth when he said, *I feel strongly that you are keeping me at arm's length, and I've felt that way for the longest time...* but if these last few days had taught her anything, it was that Bill was right, they had unfinished business, the whole family did, and if she had any hope of making amends, of finding happiness, she needed to find the courage to change, to make the leap.

As she moved her dolls and set them neatly on the chair in her bedroom, pulling back the lace counterpane and getting ready for bed, her stomach flipped with joy in antici-pation of the new life she could see waiting for her. It was all there, just for the taking! Verity was right, she just had to make herself feel good too.

Suddenly a thought came over her, an idea that ordinarily she would not have given any heed to, but this was no ordi-nary night. Pulling on her sweater, she locked the front door and, in her sneakers, crept past Mrs Kenny's home and back up the lane until she entered Town Square. Thankful for the quiet evening, and happy not to have caught the attention of the young lovers who dotted the benches, all more preoccu-pied with staring at their beau than giving her any thought at all, she reached for a pen and label from the box and leaning on the trunk of that big old tree, she wrote her wish:

'I want love, peace, and happiness... I want him to want to start over with me. I want us both to know the happiness we once did, when we were younger, and everything felt possible! I want us to grow old together, whether here in Linden Falls or anywhere else for that matter. Because I think home is where the person you love is. I don't want to run anymore...'

Vera tied her wish to the branch of the tree and crept away under the cover of the encroaching darkness, unaware that Neva and Henry had been watching her from the window of the inn.

CHAPTER 7

Three weeks later...

*V*era had lain awake until the early hours, watching the light play in patterns across her ceiling as it danced through the branches of trees and flared golden as the moon took up its place in the wings, giving the sun its chance centre stage.

She was undoubtedly tired, wanting sleep, but so nervous about the day that awaited; she tossed and turned trying to get comfortable. There was also excitement fizzing in her veins and firing her restlessness, not only at the prospect of seeing her boy and Ashley married the day after tomorrow, but also, so, so happy at the thought of seeing Bill again, knowing that her life was moving quickly, and she had to make time to live it! One thing was for sure, she wasn't getting any younger, understanding that it would only be a blink before she was sitting on the deck like Mrs Kenny, topping and tailing beans into a big old, red plastic bowl. Yes, she wanted more.

It felt good to practise in her head all the things she wanted to say to him, knowing that until she had got them off her chest, they'd sit like a boulder at the base of her throat and that wouldn't do her any good at all. But how and where to begin?

'Here's the thing, Bill, you were right what you said, you and me - we've got unfinished business...'

'Billy, I need to tell you something...'

'I don't know what the future holds, Bill, but I have to tell you that it was always you...'

'I don't have any expectations, but I've never quite gotten over you, Bill...'

'Bill, you were and are my greatest love and the fact that you gave me Knox makes it doubly special...'

'You and me, Billy, now wouldn't that be the fairytale...'

In the early hours with insects chirping in the darkness, various creatures scratching around the bin store and her cheek against the soft pillow, these thoughts and words had felt easy, possible even. Yet now as she sat on the deck, sipping her orange juice and smoothing moisturizer into her neck, the idea of saying anything remotely similar to him out loud was enough to make her gut bunch with awkwardness. Not only that, but it was Knox and Ashley's celebration, how she might or might not feel about her ex was neither here nor there in the grand scheme of things.

She hoped the weekend was going to be perfect for them. Silently she offered up a small prayer that Ashley's parents liked her, liked Linden Falls, and that they approved of the small rustic wedding that Jack and Verity were so very kindly hosting. She'd do what she always did, smile warmly, keep to chirpy chatter, and paint a verbal rainbow with her laughter, enough to glaze her world and hide the dark kernel of loneliness and inadequacy that lurked in her stomach. Unless Bill raised it first and then... well, that she'd take as a green light to Go! Go! Go! What was he'd said when he left the last time?

...I guess I'll see you in a couple of weeks. We should catch up then, properly. Finish that conversation... Try as she might to

quell her excitement, it felt almost impossible that he might not be feeling the same.

'Penny for them?' Mrs Kenny called across the way. Vera looked up, self-conscious to know the woman had probably been watching her, hoping she'd kept her thoughts as just that and not blurted them out for all to hear.

'Oh, you know, Mrs Kenny, mother of the groom nerves! I want the weekend to be perfect.'

'Well, actually I *don't* know! Mr Kenny and I were never blessed although the Good Lord knows I would have given my all to be a mother. Just never happened for us.'

'I'm sorry to hear that.' She meant it, knowing that despite the less-than-ideal circumstances and all the trials and tribulations that had come with it, being Knox's mother was the greatest thing she'd ever achieved.

'I do have the most wonderful nephew, Randall.'

'The one who installed your hot tub!'

'The very same.' The old lady smiled fondly, 'and I had Mr Kenny for nearly fifty years, God rest his soul. And he was joy enough. I miss him greatly.' Her neighbor wiped at watery eyes as if his passing and her loss was as fresh today as it had been since the day he died nearly fifteen years ago - maybe it was. Vera envied the old woman, and not for the first time that day, pictured Bill. How much time did they have left? Whatever it was, she was determined not to waste a day of it.

With the clock ticking, she got ready for the weekend, hair, make-up, best shoes, and a new pocketbook she'd picked up in town. She was all set.

'Well look at you all dressed up!' Neva called across the street as Vera walked to her truck, which she'd parked outside of the salon.

'Too much?' She ran her hands over the small frill of the pale blue linen peplum jacket that sat snuggly over the matching pencil skirt that stopped just short of her knee. She wanted to look right when greeting the small wedding party and not to be overdressed for the rehearsal dinner on the farm.

'Not at all, you look great. That waist!' Neva whistled.

It was just this kind of love and kinship that Vera valued living here in Linden Falls. She had long understood the power of women supporting and boosting other women, it created something very close to magic. Neva's comments gave her a surge of confidence.

'Thank you, Neva.'

'And bring me back some cake!'

'Will do!' She waved and jumped into her truck.

As she drove up the winding lane towards the main house at White Cedar Farm, she could see Knox on the porch, chatting to Jack and Verity. He had texted her to say they'd arrived about an hour ago.

'Mom!' He called when he saw her, putting down his cold bottle of beer and striding out to greet her.

'Well look at you! Mr soon-to-be-married man!' She took in his smart haircut and clean shave.

'You can talk, all dressed up, you look lovely.'

'Thank you, son,' as ever a compliment from him warmed her from the inside out, 'Where's Ashley?' She looked around.

'Showing her mom and dad the cabin where they'll be staying and no doubt hanging up our clothes ready for the big day, or should I say, "small day", much better...'

'You haven't changed your mind?'

Knox gave a loud, nervous laugh, 'Jeez, bit late if I had, we've got the rings engraved, the dress bought and look at how much trouble Jack and Verity have gone to... even you've gone to town! All these flowers! Can you imagine – "hey guys, I've had a change of heart!" Jeez, wouldn't that put the cat among the pigeons.' Again, he laughed.

'Knox, that's not what I meant at all!' She placed her hand

at her throat, 'I meant changed your mind about the small wedding! I knew you had big old plans at one point.'

'Oh right!' He shook his head, swallowing hard. 'No, here is as good as anywhere Mom.'

It was an odd response and lacking in the enthusiasm for the event she might have expected.

'The place looks lovely, doesn't it?'

She let her eyes rove the fresh cut flowers that filled old milk churns and galvanized buckets that she had helped Verity with only last night. They had worked and chattered, both taking great joy from the chore and each other's company with Verity ribbing her about how it might be Vera's turn next... It made her think about her wish, tied to the Linden tree, fluttering in the breeze.

'It sure does. A lot of work.' Knox nodded, pulling her from her thoughts. His gaze, she noted was off in the middle distance. 'Just got a text. Dad's about five minutes away.' He shot his cuffs and put his finger inside the collar of his shirt, as if trying to relieve some unseen pressure. She felt the roll of anticipation in her stomach, *five minutes...*

'Are you a little nervous honey?'

She noticed the slight irregular pattern to his breathing, wanting to remind him this was only a rehearsal dinner, a chance to all get to know each other and to start the cele-brations.

'About seeing Dad? No, I do it all the time.' He joked and even in this she noted the beads of sweat on his top lip.

'About getting married this weekend.' She played along.

'Oh that!' He drew a slow breath and looked out over the ridge where the slope of land dropped away and ran all the way down in a steep forest floor to the edge of the vast lake where the sun now reflected on the water, casting a glittering net over the surface. He spoke softly, 'I haven't had a single doubt, Mom. Not one.' He looked at her now, 'but yesterday and this morning? I don't know... I worry that we might be messing up what is essentially really good. We're changing something that works! And so, it feels risky.'

'It is risky, but that's marriage, right? There are never any guarantees.'

'I know that. But I want to make her happy,'

'Yes, and I want her to make *you* happy.' She interrupted, reminding him that this was his absolute right too. It was a two-way street.

He looked down as he kicked the dirt with the toe of his shoe.

'Maybe it's last-minute jitters or the realisation that we are about to make this huge commitment, but I don't want to mess up.'

'You don't need to worry about that son, you won't mess up and the fact that you're already thinking about what is best for her, for you both, means you're already right on track.'

'I guess.' He gave a wry smile, 'but I remember talking to Dad about you guys a while ago. I asked him what went wrong,' he double blinked as if a little anxious about their conversation straying into these unchartered waters.

'What did he say?' She held her breath.

'He said *nothing* went wrong.'

'He did?' She exhaled.

'Yup, he said you made choices that probably felt like the right thing at the time but that he figured you'd change your mind, but eventually he worked out that you meant what you said and that you'd gone for good.'

'He said that?' She felt a familiar mixture of sadness and excitement. Sad that Bill had never reached out, told her he was waiting for her, permission if you like for her to go back or at least to revisit, examine what had happened so long ago, and this news was bound in excitement that this might be the case, that he may in some small way, have not written them off entirely.

'Not that it matters now,' Knox dismissed the line of discussion while she was desperate to pump him for information, not that she would put her son, *their* son in that position. 'But it made me think. Dad told me he thought things were pretty good and then one day you were gone, and he was, shocked, winded. So how do I stop Ashley doing something similar, how do I keep her happy, how do I make her stay, how do I know if this is right?'

His words were the saddest confirmation of the consequences of her choices, and no matter they were made with the very best of intentions, they landed like a punch in her gut.

This was it, time to express her remorse, to come clean to her son that to leave had not been easy, but was instead a decision forged from her history, her failings, her fears, and her ragged self-esteem and how still, after all this time, she might still have feelings for Billy…

'There are reasons for the choices I made, Knox,' she began.

'Here he is!' Her son cut her short as a shiny silver hire car pulled up. 'Dad's here!'

Watching her son race towards the car, Vera felt her heart clatter in her chest.

She took a moment to pat her hair into place and to use her fingernail to run under her lower lip in case her lipstick had smudged a little. Reaching into her pocketbook, she removed the slender atomizer and as discretely at possible, spritzed her décolletage with her favoured scent. Turning to face the car, she smiled, ready to look the man in the eye who had been in her thoughts for the last three decades.

The breath caught in her throat and her knees swayed a little. She thought she might fall over, as her balance faltered and she felt the hot spread of a shameful blush, borne from pure embarrassment as it covered her chest and throat. The sight of him was entirely overwhelming. There was Bill. He looked gorgeous in his pressed slacks and smart shirt, open at the neck. He looked happy. It wasn't simply the sight of him that was overwhelming, nor was it the fact that he looked so handsome. No, it was because he looked entirely enamoured with the tall, blonde woman who was pressed close to him with her fingers tightly gripping his hand.

'There she is!' He called out, striding towards her with purpose. Vera dug deep to find a smile, lifting her trembling hand in a wave.

'Hey!' She called as the two were upon her in seconds.

The woman was pretty, about her age, if she'd had to guess, and dressed in a short dress with a peplum not dissimilar to her own but in a shade of baby pink that suited her colouring. She was smiling broadly, confidently, and Vera wanted the ground to open up and swallow her whole.

'V, so good to see you!' He leaned forward to kiss her on the cheek, still with his hand firmly gripping that of his guest.

'Good... good to see you too,' she managed from a mouth sticky with nerves.

'This is Sandrine.' He turned to face the woman briefly, speaking her name like he was announcing her on a stage. 'Sandrine, this is V who I've told you all about.'

In this, Sandrine had the advantage. Vera remembered to close her mouth which wanted to gape in shock.

'So nice to meet you V,' the woman used the nickname that was special, that had been special to the two of them. It bothered her far more than it should.

'Nice... nice to meet you too.' She stuttered.

'Billy this place is amazing!' The woman turned almost full circle and marvelled at the sights from the vantage point at the top of the driveway. 'He told me it was pretty but didn't do it justice! This is just darlin'! And you live here, V?'

'Not far.'

'Oh yes, Ash said.'

Billy... Ash... This woman was no temporary fixture. And in that moment, Vera, the little girl who had grown up with fairy tales dancing behind her eyelids every night in the warm cocoon of southern heat, saw the dream of reconciliation drift away like a petal on the breeze...

'Those two, go together like peas and carrots, don't they?' Sandrine's laugh was again raucous.

'They do. Where're you from?' Vera knew the accent was not Ithaca based.

'Tennessee, you know it?'

'Long time ago.' She nodded.

Knox walked over with a suitcase, 'So Mom, I told you it was hard getting Dad to agree to a date with Melissa from the admin dept? Well, turns out he was being evasive as he was hiding Sandrine away!'

'Hardly hidin' darlin! You can hear me laughing all the way across town!'

Vera didn't doubt it.

'We didn't want to say anything until we knew we had something to say. But this was what I wanted to talk to you about V, without stealing Knox' thunder of course!' Bill beamed at the woman with a look of pure love that was a dagger to Vera's heart.

'So, you haven't only known each other for three weeks?' She was doing the math, trying to work out the last time she had seen Bill.

Sandrine again boomed that laugh, 'Good Lord above no! We've been off and on and on and off for little over a year now. And now we're finally on!' Sandrine raised the third finger on her left hand to show the large baguette cut diamond and emerald ring, one she recognized as belonging to Bill's grandmother. She was sure she gasped out loud and instantly put her hand over her mouth, hoping the assembled might think it was in awe of the pretty, antique ring.

The day he tried to give it to her was etched in her mind,

'*Please V, just put it on your finger! Put it on your finger and at least think about it!*' He had pleaded, as she pushed it back over the small table in their kitchen with Knox asleep in his cot in the next room.

'*I don't need to think about it! I aint the marryin' kind!*'

'*Well maybe you weren't but then you met me!*' He had laughed.

'*You think I say no lightly? Knowing what everyone at church thinks about me being a mom but not a wife? You think any of this is funny William?*'

He had rolled over laughing, '*Well now I do because you are calling me William.*' He'd reached up and pulled her down onto his lap. '*You'll change your mind; you'll marry me one day!*' He had kissed her firmly on the mouth and the two had taken advantage of the fact that Knox slept soundly, and they were alone.

Well, she had come close to changing her mind, and look where that had got her, all too late. All much, much too late...

'This is what I wanted to talk to you about V, this is my unfinished business. I couldn't wait to tell you all about her.'

'Look at his face, like a possum eatin' sweet tater!' Sandrine laughed again and kissed Bill right on the cheek.

'Get a room!' It was Ashley that called out as she made her way up the hill. And Bill and his fiancé sprang apart, but still kept those hands tightly wound together, she noticed.

'Hey Vera!'

'Hello Sweetie!' She gratefully accepted the hug from the girl and made eye contact with the two rather sheepish onlookers standing behind her. Both dressed in shades of grey, with grey hair and grey skin. 'These are my parents, Miko and Andrew.'

Andrew with a boat...

'How do you do.' Andrew stepped forward and shook her hand solemnly. She noted his palm was dry, his mouth thin, as Sandrine again laughed,

'"*How do you do?*" My goodness, if I'd known I was in such fine company I'd have put my good teeth in!'

Bill's laughter burst from him, and she too raised a smile, knowing without doubt that in any other situation, in any other life, at any other moment, she would like Sandrine. She would like her a lot.

Vera shook hands with Ashley's mother who very much like Andrew was a little formal. It was about as far from the warm interaction of newly introduced soon to be in-laws that she could envisage. Verity's voice was a welcome distraction for them all.

'Good evening, everyone!' She locked eyes with Vera, having obviously seen Bill hand in hand with Sandrine. Vera did her best to keep her reaction subtle, whilst acknowledging her friend's awareness. 'Please do all make your way up to the top terrace where dinner is going to be served.'

'Verity is the one I told you about,' Ashley enthused, 'she used to be married to Sonny Joseph – who has *two* Michelin stars? We walked past their place when we were in Chelsea.'

'Oh! Yes, I remember!' Her mum's face lit up for the first time and it bothered Vera that it was this fact Ashley had chosen to recount about her generous host, when Jack had been so accommodating, so wonderful. There was also the slight feeling of inadequacy that it was Verity who had been recommended, spoken about.

'Yup, that's me! Sonny Joseph's ex-wife!' Verity pulled a face and turned on her heel. She sincerely hoped her friend wasn't already regretting offering to hold the wedding weekend here, if she was, it was going to be a very long couple of days...

Vera walked up the hill towards the top terrace, fighting the desire to vomit. She hated how this time of celebration was being hijacked by her feelings of envy and distress that fought for pole position, noting how Bill guided Sandrine with his hand on the small of her back while she took great caution not to stumble on her heels.

'Isn't she great?' He asked over his shoulder like a kid with a shiny new thing.

'She sure is!' She managed, even though her gut folded with something that felt a lot like loss.

Of course, she knew before they last met that it was possible he'd have moved on, they'd been apart for over a decade, but Knox's words had made her think he was single right now and to look at Sandrine, meant all her worst fears were confirmed. Bill looked so very happy, and he was with a smart, sassy, fun woman who reminded Vera so powerfully of herself it was hard to swallow. Not that she had a tenth of the woman's confidence. When Knox had told her that he was struggling to fix a date for Bill and Melissa she'd been shocked to feel so excited, as if a door she had believed to be closed was open again, or if not open entirely, then certainly not padlocked shut.

And only this morning, she had been desperate to see the man again. The man who was calm, the man with the salt and pepper beard who had made her feel safe each night as he climbed onto their insubstantial mattress in his student digs. The man who was engaged, it seemed to Sandrine, Sandrine who now wore the ring she had declined.

CHAPTER 8

*T*he dinner was a little quiet. Andrew and Miko it seemed, preferred to talk to each other in hushed tones rather than join in the chat that bounced back and forth across the table between Knox, Ashley, Knox's friend Jesse and Ashley's best friend Marianne. Verity and Jack too were invited, and she was in awe of how they kept the event moving, pouring wine, joining in as Jesse drank more and more and his toasts became ever more elaborate.

Once or twice, she spied Knox, looking a little pensive, smiling widely for sure but it was a smile that didn't seem to reach his eyes. Bill and Sandrine sat very closely together, and she couldn't stop watching them. It was similar to driving past an accident, knowing the best thing to do would be to look away, to not put the haunting images into her head, but at the same time she was powerfully drawn, stealing glances whenever the opportunity arose. It was her own private torture. Staring as Sandrine raked her nails on the back of his neck as they both listened to Andrew sharing a very dull story about tide times in the Hamptons. And then the way Bill had tucked a stray lock of her hair behind her ear and the two had kissed, gently and quickly with noses bumping, as if the act was still new and all-consuming and the look of bliss on their faces suggesting that to kiss was the thing that made them happy. The happiest.

It was all she could do not to grab her new pocketbook and run! And if it wasn't for the fact they were there to celebrate Knox and Ashley, and she was wearing shoes that were highly inappropriate for running, she might have. Her heart felt like an overly ripe pomegranate, threatening to burst open at any second. Envy coated her tongue with a bitterness that turned all she ate to ashes in her mouth.

Verity, her lovely friend in whom she had confided, kept checking on her, offering lingering looks of solace, winks when appropriate and small nods of encouragement. Vera was thankful, as ever for both her concern and her love. A small part of her wished she hadn't been so open about her feelings where Bill was concerned, knowing she would now have to deal with the embarrassment of reneging on her admission and the pasting over her words with platitudes that she hoped might mask her hurt.

It was a little before ten o'clock that Jesse and Marianne disappeared from the table, much to the amusement of Knox and Ashley who had apparently predicted this might happen. Ashley then went back to the car to find a sweater. Andrew and Miko had politely called it a night, creeping off into the darkness in the same shy way they'd arrived. Sandrine and Bill stood to dance cheek to cheek to the soft music that flowed around them, slow and low country - courtesy of Jack's sound system. Verity gathered plates and dishes, all scraped clean of the wonderful food she'd provided, ready to ferry them inside. String lights provided starlight-like light that doused every image in muted golden tones that gave the whole evening an ethereal quality. Vera knew that if her heart were not weeping, cleaved in two, it would have been some night.

'I'll come help you.' She placed her napkin on the table

and grabbed a wooden board where chunks of soft, rosemary and garlic studded, homemade focaccia had lurked only hours before.

'No! I've got it! You sit and chat to your boy.' Verity insisted, nodding towards Knox who stared into space.

Vera walked to his end of the table and took the chair only recently vacated by her future daughter-in-law.

'Penny for your thoughts?' She leaned her head on her elbow with her back to Bill and his fiancée. Her son looked towards her, and his expression might best be described as a little wine fuddled. 'You want a coffee honey?' She figured this might be wise.

Knox leant forward and spoke quietly, 'I don't want,' he shook his head. 'I don't,'

Sensing his struggle to get the words out, she intervened, 'you don't want a coffee?' Using the tone she used to coax mac and cheese into his mouth when he was being stubborn, to encourage him to turn the lights out on a school night and to convince him that it was going to be okay, *you're going to live with your dad and he's a pretty awesome guy...*

Knox shook his head, 'No Mom. I don't... I don't want to get married.'

His voice was quiet, controlled and yet his eyes were wide and fearful. His skin had taken on the pale khaki hue of the slightly inebriated.

'What's that now?' Confident she had heard him correctly, she needed it repeating because if he had said what she was sure he *had* said, then this would require all of her attention.

'I said,' he swallowed and looked her in the eye, 'I said I don't want to get married.'

'That's what I thought.' Reaching for his hand, she gripped it tightly, wanting him to know that no matter what, he was supported. 'Are you sure?'

He chewed his bottom lip. 'You need to be a hundred

percent sure right, Mom? On things like this, things as important as marriage?'

'I'd say hundred is quite high. Maybe eight nine. Eighty nine percent is a good bench mark. No one can ever be one hundred even if they try and convince themselves that they are.'

'I guess I'm about sixty percent right now.' He levelled.

'Okay.' She looked over at Bill and Sandrine who she would put at about ninety-nine, while her heart lurched for her son who was in a tricky situation. Her pulse raced as she thought about Ashley and her dry parents who at that very minute were probably going about their night time rituals, checking tide times or whatever they did before bed. She might have had slight reservations about the girl, but this was not a situation she would have wished on any of them. 'Sixty is not really enough.'

'That's what I figured.' He wiped his face with his palms and closed his eyes for a second, as if resetting, taking stock, understanding that the genie was out of the bottle. 'I like what we have, I like her, I *love* her! But,'

'But what?' She urged.

'I don't know if it's a forever kind of love or a right now kind of love.'

'There's a big difference.' She confirmed. 'Wanting to hang out with someone be with them, sleep with them and all that fun, is one thing, but a commitment like marriage? It isn't something you should do lightly, you're right. It wouldn't be fair on either of you.'

'Knox?' Ashley called from the shadows and came slowly into view, her hands knitted, fingers fidgeting, and she had clearly been crying.

'Yes?' He swung around in the chair and the two held each other's gaze.

Vera couldn't have said who cried first but as Knox rose

and the two ran to each other there were certainly tears aplenty.

'I'm sorry!' Ashley spoke through her distress. 'I'm not ready. I love you; I do. I love you so much!' Her words were hard and sincere. 'But I'm not ready. Do you understand where I'm coming from? I don't want to lose you, but marriage?'

Knox held her tightly and looked at his mom over her shoulder, 'I do.' He smiled warmly as he ran his hand over her hair, 'I do.'

IT HAD BEEN QUITE A NIGHT. Vera kissed Knox and Ashley good bye and thanked Verity and Jack for their hospitality.

'Want to take some wedding cake with you?' Verity offered, half joking, as they had two tiers of fine gateaux chocolat to get through, what with the fact that there was not going to be a wedding after all.

'No, but I reckon Neva and Henry might like a slice!' She suggested.

Miko and Andrew had slept through the whole revelatory evening, and she wondered how they would take it in the morning when Ashley broke the news. Not overly distressed, would be her accurate guess.

Letting her truck navigate the way home, she thought again of Bill and Sandrine, who had both hugged her warmly when she left and insisted she agree to come to their wedding wherever and whenever that might be. She had nodded and promised to do her best to make that happen, but with her fingers crossed behind her brand-new handbag. Being friendly and supportive was one thing, but attending their wedding? She shook her head.

The town square was quiet, bar the rustle of leaves in the tree and the dance of the wishes that hung from its branches tied on ribbons. The pretty lights all around the edge made the place feel welcoming and the air was warm. Vera pulled up, parked the truck, and ditched her heels, throwing them into the backseat. Walking barefoot over the grass, she came to rest at the base of the tree where Verity and Jack had seen her folded with loss on that Christmas night. Looking up she spoke firmly,

'I just came to say that I'm done with wishing. Why can't I catch a break? I even practised what I was going to say to Bill like an idiot! But no more.' Tentatively, she placed her hand on its wide trunk. 'No more wishing. No more day dreamin' about all I don't have and all I'll never have. Love, peace, and happiness? I'm done thinking that you, you big old stoopid tree might make a difference! Instead, I'm going to grab this life and make it my own! I'm not leaving Linden Falls, I'm not going to cut and run, not this time. This is my home, it's where my friends are and where my business is and where I am loved! And I *am* loved. No one here sees me as that skinny old Delaney kid and it's time I started to see myself like that too. Women like Sandrine, they're not hiding away, wishing things were different – they are courageous and that's what I need, courage!'

Standing, she walked to underside of the grand tree and reached up onto the lower branch where she'd tied her wish with gold and there it was,

...I want him to want to start over with me. I want us to both know the happiness we did, when we were young, and everything felt possible! I want us to grow old together, whether here in Linden Falls or anywhere else for that matter. Because I think home is where the person you love is. I don't want to run anymore...

Taking it into her hands, she ripped it once, twice, then three times before shoving it into her handbag.

'Yep, I'm done with wishing.' This she threw over her shoulder as she made her way back to her truck.

It was a month later that Vera pulled the pale envelope from the dark confines of her mailbox; she stopped short on the path. Her heart raced and the breath stuttered in her throat. She read and re-read the return address,

'Ithaca,' it could only mean one thing, *Knox*. Exhaling slowly, her face broke into a smile at the sound of his name in her thoughts. Popping the letter into her purse, she decided to open it at work while the tea kettle boiled, giving her time to savour every written word, every dot, and every dash, before her first customer of the day.

'Morning Mrs Kenny!' She waved.

'Well, someone got out of the right side of the bed this morning!'

Vera laughed and made her way into town. She was early but wanted to open up the salon and read her letter before Mira pitched up.

With the lights of the salon now gleaming and the blinds pulled up to let the day in, Vera took a minute in the back to grab the letter from her purse. Leaning on the small sink, she slowly placed the envelope under her nose and inhaled. It was then that she heard the tinkle of the little bell above the door and popping the letter into her pocket for safe keeping, she walked into the salon and stopped in her tracks.

She stood still while her heart settled and took a deep breath hoping her breathing might find its natural rhythm. It would have been hard to describe what was happening to her, but it was a lot like being hit by a thunderbolt. The man was tall and had shoulder length dark hair, his face was cracked in an easy smile and his hazel eyes stared at her, in a way that was familiar and warming.

'Huh?' He asked, and it took a minute for her to follow his thread.

'What?

'Did you not ask me something?' She liked his Southern drawl.

'Not as I recall...' She smiled.

'Oh,' he walked forward, and she bunched her fists, to stop from reaching out to touch him right there and then.

'Neva said I needed a haircut. And so here I am.' He ran his fingers through his hair.

'Neva?'

'Yes.' She came into my gallery and said that no self-respecting business owner would have hair this messy. He shrugged.

'Neva?' she smiled.

'Yes.'

'And you are?'

'Wyatt. Just moved here. I'm a friend of Jacks.'

'You're Wyatt?' she smiled.

'I am.'

'Well, take a seat, Wyatt, and let's see what we can do with that hair....'

EPILOGUE

*V*era locked her front door and popped her key in her purse. It was a cool morning with a hint of pink lurking in the sky that might mean warmth later. She hoped so. Mrs Kenny was on the deck, looking out over the lane with a mug of tea in her palms.

'Morning Mrs Kenny!'

'Morning dear.' The woman did a double take. 'Hope you don't mind me saying, Vera, but what in the name of God have you done to your hair?'

'You like it?' She patted the pin curls that hung down around her slender neck, aware of the bouffant poodle effect that sat in a heap on top. The shade had been described on the side of the bottle as lavender honey, but the effect was more summer sky blue. Yep, no doubt about it, it was definitely blue.

'You did that on purpose?' The woman stared and her mouth fell open a little. It did little to give Vera confidence that this latest look was a good idea. Not that it mattered, she could easily fix it with a new colour any time she chose.

'I did indeed.' She beamed her megawatt smile and walked along the track with a spring in her step.

Linden Falls was waking up, the curbs were being swept, folks queued for coffee, while others jogged with those little ear bud thingies in that Vera did not understand how they worked, where was the music coming from and why didn't they fall out? She'd have to ask Knox who might reply, if he wasn't too busy painting the nursery. A grandchild! She couldn't wait. Miko and Andrew had even thawed a little and seemed to be excited, happy too that the youngsters had finally tied the knot at the court house. No fuss, no guests, no fancy frock, or flowers. But confirmed via a picture taken on the steps, the two looking so very happy and with an accompanying text from Knox that only she knew the true meaning of.

We did it Mom! Love Knox. 99.9999%

She was still waiting for an invite from Bill and Sandrine.

Walking swiftly, she raised her hand in response to the various calls of 'Mornin' Vera!' shouted from cars as they passed and shop doors, as the proprietors got ready for the day ahead. The joyful anticipation she felt at putting her key in the door and walking inside her own premises would never diminish. It might only be a small salon in a quiet town, but it was quite a thing for a woman like her to be a business owner. And what a pretty little business it was. Letting her eyes rove the mirrors and basins, all just so, and awaiting her customers for the day, she felt a warm satisfaction in her bones. This was hers, and she had done it all by herself.

Mira was going to be in late, she had a dental appointment, and it was as Vera studied the appointment book that the little bell over the front door heralded an arrival.

'Hey Pam! Nice to see you!'

Pam Olson was not one of Vera's more daring clients, on account of her long, thick dark hair, which she nearly always wore in a ponytail. It was, nonetheless, always good to see her.

'Nice to see you too.' Pam put her bag on the floor and took her regular seat in front of the mirror. 'And wow! You are looking blue! In a good way.'

'You think it's too much?' Vera looked over her shoulder into the mirror, wondering if she had gone full smurf.

'I like it!'

Vera squeezed her shoulder in gratitude.

'Well, I like it too. And you Ms Olson are looking gooooood!'

It was hard not to admire the fantastic figure of the woman.

'Well, I wouldn't be a very good advert as a personal trainer if I didn't work out now, would I?' Pam laughed, but Vera could tell she was pleased with the compliment.

'So, how's things?' Pam beamed, toying with the ends of her hair as if already concerned with having too much cut off. This was quite common with those who had long, gorgeous hair.

'How's things?' Vera thought how best to answer, how had things been in the few months since she'd last cut Pam's hair?

Well, my son and his fiancée turned up quite suddenly and we had an interesting few days to put it mildly, then they came back mere weeks later and nearly got married but my son got cold feet, which I kind of think is for the best, as his fiancée got cold feet too! Oh, and I decided to make my feelings known to the man I thought was the love of my life who it turned out had already found the love of his life and it isn't me... My son and his fiancé decided they did want to marry after all and did so in haste and are now expecting a baby! Yes, I'm going to be a meemaw! Mira is at a dental appointment, and tonight I get to go home to a wonderful meal cooked for me by a tall, dark, handsome stranger called Wyatt who frames pictures for a living. Although he's not so strange to me now. And even though it's only been a few months, I have the oddest feeling that it might just be a forever kind of love and not a right now kind of love. I think that about sums it up!

'Things are good! Real good. I'm happy. Very happy.' She chose to answer with this, positive, and upbeat as ever. Living as she did in this state of love, peace, and happiness.

'You certainly look it.' Pam nodded at her knowingly. Both women it seemed had lived and loved and both knew how hard it was when a love life was the opposite of smooth sailing.

'And how's it going with Steve?'

Pam's face lit up at the mention of her man. 'It's going so well, sometimes it scares me. I keep thinking he can't be this wonderful, can he? There's got to be something he's hiding.'

Vera laughed out loud. 'I know that feeling or at least I did. I always used to jump, or more accurately run, before I was pushed or before someone let me down. But in truth Pam, the only person who suffered, was me. So don't doubt, don't over-question, just enjoy the moment!'

'I'll think about that Vera.' Her words had clearly resonated. 'And I certainly have time to think. Now that I've finished renovating my house, I'm at loose ends. I need another big project - I just don't know what it'll be. But I have this strange feeling that something big is right around the corner...'

Vera sure knew that feeling. Bill had been wrong when he suggested she'd be heading out sometime soon, reminding her of all the times she had cut and run, but not this time. This was where she belonged. This place right here. She had built a better world, where she could be a better person; a person who had rid herself of the stink of her dysfunctional family, a person who was loved, and a person who, on good days, even loved herself.

Both women smiled, as if ready for whatever adventure awaited them, here in Linden Falls, the place they called home...

To discover what's next, read <u>WISHES OF HOME</u>, the next book in series by Barbara Hanse.

Don't miss any books in the Wishing Tree series:

★ Don't miss a Wishing Tree book! ★
Book 1: The Wishing Tree – prologue book
Book 2: I Wish.. by Amanda Prowse
Book 3: Wish You Were Here by Kay Bratt
Book 4: Wish Again by Tammy L. Grace
Book 5: Workout Wishes & Valentine Kisses by Barbara Hinske
Book 6: A Parade of Wishes by Camille Di Maio
Book 7: Careful What You Wish by Ashley Farley
Book 8: Gone Wishing by Jessie Newton
Book 9: Wishful Thinking by Kay Bratt
Book 10: Overdue Wishes by Tammy L. Grace
Book 11: A Whole Heap of Wishes by Amanda Prowse
Book 12: Wishes of Home by Barbara Hinske
Book 13: Wishful Witness by Tonya Kappes

WE ALSO INVITE you to join us in our My Book Friends group on Facebook. It's a great place to chat about all things bookish and learn more about our founding authors.

FROM THE AUTHOR

Dear reader,

Linden Falls is a genteel place, somewhere I go to forget my worries and catch-up with old friends. I hope it's the same for you.

As an author, it has been a huge privilege to work so closely with all of these incredible other women who have written books in the series, creating a neighborhood, a wonderful world that we can visit.

I hope that you, like me, have enjoyed spending time in Linden Falls with Vera and the other residents. I love it when different characters pop up in each other's stories, just like in real life when sometimes you bump into your neighbor in a store and get the opportunity to have a catch up.

By reading every book in the Wishing Tree series you will, become part of the community and be able to follow the daily lives of the townsfolk there. To find out more about the latest developments, please head over to Linden Falls and keep in touch with your friends.

Much love,

Amanda Xx

ABOUT THE AUTHOR

Amanda Prowse is an International Bestselling author whose twenty-eight novels, two non-fiction titles and eight novellas have been published in dozens of languages around the world. Published by Lake Union, Amanda is the most prolific writer of bestselling contemporary fiction in the UK today and her titles also consistently score the highest online review approval ratings across several genres. Her books, including the chart-topping No.1 titles 'What Have I Done?', 'Perfect Daughter', 'My Husband's Wife', 'The Girl in the Corner' and 'The Things I Know' have sold millions of copies across the globe.

A popular TV and radio personality, Amanda has appeared on numerous shows where her views on family and social issues strike a chord with viewers. She also makes countless guest appearances on BBC national and independent Radio stations including LBC, Times Radio and Talk FM, where she is well known for her insightful observations and her infectious humour. Described by the Daily Mail as 'The queen of family drama' Amanda's novel, 'A Mother's Story' won the coveted Sainsbury's eBook of the year Award and she has had two books selected as World Book Night titles, 'Perfect Daughter' in 2016 and 'The Boy Between' in 2022.

Amanda is a huge supporter of libraries and having become a proud ambassador for The Reading Agency, works tirelessly to promote reading, especially in disadvantaged areas. Amanda's ambition is to create stories that keep people from turning the bedside lamp off at night, great characters that ensure you take every step with them and tales that fill your head so you can't possibly read another book until the memory fades...

You can get in touch with Amanda via any of the social media platforms below and if you would like to find out a bit more about her other works, please visit her website, or Author Pages on Amazon or Goodreads

Say hello on Twitter: @MrsAmandaProwse

Friend me on Facebook: www.facebook.com/Amanda-ProwseAuthor

Tag me on Instagram: www.instagram.com/MrsAman-daProwse

Check out my website: www.amandaprowse.com

Made in United States
North Haven, CT
30 September 2022

24743612R00071